Mantras

Sacred Words of Power

Mantras
Sacred Words of Power

JOHN BLOFELD

*A Dutton
Paperback*

E. P. DUTTON

NEW YORK

This paperback edition of

MANTRAS: SACRED WORDS OF POWER

First published 1977 by E. P. Dutton & Co., Inc.

Library of Congress Catalog Card Number: 76-52321

ISBN: 0-525-47451-X

10 9 8 7 6 5 4 3 2

First Edition

To Lu K'uan-yü (Charles Luk)
to whom the Western world owes much for
his lucid renderings of Chinese works
containing treasures of Buddhist and
Taoist wisdom

Author's Preface

How strangely things come together! Again and again one stumbles upon a word or thought long out of mind only to find it re-echoed perhaps twice or thrice within the space of a few days. Several years ago I toyed with and then discarded the idea of writing a book on mantras. It would not do, I felt, to expose sacred matters to possible derision or lightly set aside the safeguards wherewith mantric knowledge has been guarded from profanation throughout the centuries. In the last few years, however, circumstances have altered. The interest in Eastern wisdom now displayed by thousands of young people in the West is genuine and not wanting in reverence; unlike their elders and forefathers, they do not deride what is mysterious merely because it does not accord with the categories of Western scientific thought. This change of attitude deserves and has received a warm response; nowadays even the most conservative upholders of Eastern traditions are inclined to relax the rigour of ancient safeguards out of compassion for those whose desire for wisdom is sincere but who are unable to journey far from home and sit at the feet of the wise for years on end. No sooner had a series of apparently disconnected incidents caused me to ponder anew the implications of this change than a letter arrived from that outstanding authority and writer on Chinese Buddhism, Lu K'uan-yü (Charles Luk), urging me to set about writing exactly the kind of work I had once had in mind.

My first reaction was cautious. I replied that I felt hesitant on account of the *samaya*-vows which enjoin discretion in regard to all knowledge to which access is attained through tantric initiation; for, though my lama, the Venerable Dodrup Chen, has given me permission to write whatever I deem fitting, I am naturally reluctant to make decisions in such a matter. Then came another letter from Lu K'uan-yü to the same effect as the first. After mulling over his suggestion, I accepted it, but with a self-imposed proviso – that is to say, I decided to confine myself to speaking of mantras which, having already appeared in published works, must certainly be known to (and perhaps misunderstood by) the uninitiated. Thus I hoped to avoid making unwarrantable disclosures and, at the same time, to clear up some probable misconceptions.

Following the general line of approach taken in my earlier books on similar subjects, I have begun at what for me personally was the beginning, by relating more or less chronologically my early encounters with mantric practice. Hence the first two or three chapters have no profundity, though I hope they will be found entertaining. Readers who, hitherto, have equated mantras with magic spells or mumbo-jumbo will find that this was nearly my own position at the start, although faith in the wisdom of my Chinese friends prevented me from closing my mind against what might seem to me nonsense, even if they thought otherwise. I hope I shall succeed in kindling a reverence for mantric arts and belief in their validity just as my own were kindled – step by step.

I should like to stress that I happened upon mantras, rather than came upon them by design. Although my interest in them, once aroused, was perfectly sincere, I made no search for mantric knowledge and what I acquired of it was incidental to my quest for yogas whereby Enlightenment might be achieved, of which mantras sometimes form a part. I have been exceedingly fortunate in meeting men of wisdom and true sanctity both Chinese and Tibetan, many of them well-versed in mantric lore, but I am very far from having achieved a mastery of the subject. That I have dared to write about it is not because I know much, but because many others, lacking my opportunities, may be presumed to know even less. To this day – as the reader will discover towards the end – there are aspects of mantras that remain as mysterious to me as ever. In my own mind, I divide mantras into three categories of which I feel able to speak with some slight authority only on the first:

1 Mantras used in yogic contemplation, which are marvellous but not miraculous.
2 Mantras with effects that are seemingly miraculous.

3 Mantras which, if the claims made for them are valid, must
  provisionally be deemed to operate miraculously, at least until the manner of their operation is better understood.

Most of what follows the two or three introductory chapters
concerns yogic contemplation. Though this may be thought the
least spectacular aspect of mantras, it alone is of ultimate importance.

I am grateful to Lu K'uan-yü for his encouragement; to the
Lama Anagarika Govinda for a letter that, taken in conjunction
with his published writings, solved several problems for me;
to my good friend, Gerald Yorke, for information about the
Hindu theory of mantric power as well as about several Western
practices analogous to the use of mantras; and to Dom Sylvester
Houédard of Prinknash Abbey for the voluminous scholarly
notes from which I culled my references to the Jesus Prayer
and the Ismu'z Zat of the Sufis.

JOHN BLOFELD,
The House of Wind and Cloud

Contents

Author's Preface   *page* ix
1 The Forest of Recluses   1
2 The Lost Tradition   15
3 The Beginning of Understanding   31
4 The Indwelling Deity   50
5 Some Yogic Mantras   69
6 Words of Power   83
7 Shabda, Sacred Sound   96

Illustrations

between pages 46-47

1 The Twenty-One Taras
2 Shakyamuni Buddha
3 Yamāntaka
4 Avalokiteshvara
  The White Tara
5 The Precious Guru (in youthful guise)
  The Precious Guru (in characteristic guise)
6 Manjushri
7 Amitayus Buddha
8 Tara's Mantra

Mantras
Sacred Words of Power

Chapter 1

The Forest of Recluses

It was like a dream. Within the wide chamber, though the candle-rays reflected by the chalices and ritual implements assembled upon the altar glittered like silver fire and though the painted mandala of deities rising behind it contained every imaginable hue, the prevailing light was pale gold – the colour of the rice-straw matting that ran from wall to wall, its immaculate surface broken only by the low, square blackwood altar and the rows of bronze-coloured meditation cushions. The cushions were now occupied. But for the motion of their lips and of their breathing, the white-robed figures resembled statues, so profound was the tranquillity conjured up by the deep-toned syllables that, regulated by the drum's majestic rhythm, welled sonorously from their lips.

LOMAKU SICHILIA JIPIKIA NAN SALABA TATA-GEATA NAN. ANG BILAJI BILAJI MAKASA GEYALA SATA SATA SARATÉ SARATÉ TALAYI TALAYI BIDAMANI SANHANJIANI TALAMACHI SIDA GRIYA *TALANG* SOHA!

Presently I came to know that not one of the devotees, though their minds responded to the enchantment without fail, knew the meaning of those syllables whose sound was more inspiring than a solemn paean! The language was not their native Cantonese; nor, despite having been transmitted to their teacher by his Master in Japan, was it Japanese; nor yet medieval Chinese, though the mantra had reached Japan from China a thousand years before; nor was it Sanskrit – but rather Sanskrit modified down the centuries and by a whole series of transitions. Strangely, none of this mattered, for the syllables of a mantra, even should they happen to be intelligible, owe nothing of their power to meaning at the level of conceptual thought. Here was the beginning of a mystery to which I was thenceforth to devote almost life-long attention. Now, after four decades, I cannot truly say that I have solved it!

When, as a youth, I first set out for China, sudden illness compelled me to disembark at Hong Kong. There circumstances led to my remaining for a year or more, cultivating the friendship of a group of conservatively minded Chinese who fondly clung to the ancient wisdom and traditions of their race. Among them was a physician of the old school, a pale-faced scholar in his early thirties who, disdaining Western fashions, wore a skull-cap of stiff black satin topped by a scarlet bobble and, in summer, a thin white silken gown that was ankle-length and had a high, upstanding collar. In winter the gown was replaced by one of thicker silk, dark-coloured and warmly padded with silk-floss, over which he often wore a formal Manchu jacket of black, figured satin. As proclaimed by his appearance, Dr Tsai Ta-hai was a man of tradition through and through – not a lover of fossilised Confucian rigidity, but imbued by the spirit at once humanist, mystical and playful that characterises the choicest Chinese poetry and painting. Deeply learned in Taoist and Buddhist lore, he was steeped in the mystery of the myriad ever-changing forms permeated by the formless, self-perpetuating, unchanging Tao which is so cunningly delineated in old poems and landscapes. When we first met, he was enthusiastic about an esoteric form of Buddhism no longer current in China which, in a somewhat truncated form, had survived in Japan from where it had recently been transmitted to a group of Buddhist devotees in Hong Kong.

Our friendship, which was to be cemented years later by an oath of brotherhood, blossomed magically from the evening of our first encounter. In another book, *The Wheel of Life*, I have described at greater length how, laid low by intermittent fever, I sent my 12-year-old Cantonese serving-lad to find a doctor; and how this child, knowing nothing of a foreigner's preferences, ran to the nearest – Dr Tsai Ta-hai, a Chinese herbalist, who, though surprised at being summoned by a 'foreign devil', came at once and, touching his slender fingers to each of my wrists in turn, felt not for one but for six pulses! His method of diagnosis was no less astonishing to a young man fresh from England; it consisted of plunging his mind into inner stillness and silently intuiting the disturbances to my body's rhythms. The prescription he wrote in beautiful calligraphy with the set of writing implements that formed the most essential part of his portable medical equipment, led to the purchase of many small packets of strange substances which, boiled together, produced a thin, black, bitter liquid with amazing healing properties. Discovering that I was a Buddhist, he questioned me with delighted astonishment. I shall never forget the joy that lit his face on learning that, for the first time in his life, he had come upon a Westerner who was eager to learn from the Chinese instead of being determined to impose Western ways upon them.

As soon as I was fit again, my new friend took me to a gathering in a house which, as proclaimed by a horizontal lacquer board above the entrance, was curiously named 'The Forest of Recluses'. It was in fact a kind of private temple belonging to an association of Buddhist laymen. I was informed that nearly every city in China had its Forest of Recluses, but that this one was unusual in that its members espoused a form of Buddhism which, having died out in China a thousand years ago, survived in Japanese form as the Shingon Sect. The resident teacher, Lai Fa-shih (Dharma-Master Lai), after passing some years in retreat on Mount Koya not very far from Kyoto, had returned from Japan to instruct his fellow-Chinese in what remained of the secret lore that had prevailed among their ancestors in the days when the Esoteric Sect (Mi Tsung) still flourished. Shingon, like its Tibetan counterpart, the Vajrayana or Mantrayana, safeguards its yogic secrets from profanation by confining instruction to initiates. It was by the special courtesy of Ta-hai's friends that the English youth Ah Jon, as they called me, was permitted to attend and even participate in the rites, though lacking as yet even a preliminary initiation. The kindness of those people was beyond belief.

Standing upon a slight eminence near Causeway Bay in what was then a partly rural area, the Forest of Recluses was an ordinary looking house more Western than Chinese in style. Most of its rooms, to which were attached broad, glazed verandas, were like those to be found in many middle-class Hong Kong dwellings of that period; but on the upper floor was the beautiful chamber I have described, always fragrant with the scent of sandalwood incense. Behind the altar with its elaborate set of silver furnishings rose several painted panels, of which the central one depicted nine 'meditation Buddhas and Bodhisattvas' seated in the centre and on the petals of a lotus. These and the figures on the subsidiary panels were wrought in bright fresh colours and markedly similar in style to the exquisite frescoes one sees upon the walls of ancient Buddhist cave-temples in China, India and Ceylon. The likeness was not confined to the arrangement, postures and symbolism, but arose chiefly from the sublime expressions and airy delicacy of the figures – those borne upon clouds seemed truly ethereal and those with wings to be truly flying. Iconographically, the central panel closely resembled one form of the Tibetan mandala. Seated in the centre of the lotus was Vairochana Buddha; four other meditation Buddhas depicting Wisdom–Compassion Energies occupied the petals corresponding to the main compass points and four Bodhisattvas were seated on the alternating petals. Struck by the beauty of this arrangement, I had as yet no notion of its esoteric significance. Thinking back to it, I cannot doubt the common ancestry of the Japanese Shingon and Tibetan Vajrayana sects, although the former preserves only a small part of that heritage.

As a newcomer, drawn to China by admiration of the beauty and wisdom I had gleaned from Waley's and Obata's translations of Chinese poetry and from rather similar sources, I was eager to enjoy whatever experiences my Chinese friends had to offer; so I fell in easily with their ways, doing uncritically whatever they suggested and leaving understanding to dawn later. One or two evenings a week, we would assemble on an enclosed veranda adjoining the shrine-room, the others dressed in Chinese gowns worn over loose silk trousers, myself in the suits I had brought from England, of which the trousers proved woefully unsuited to sitting cross-legged on a cushion for the duration of the rites. Soon I began coming to the house with a pair of silk trousers wrapped in a parcel so that I could change into them when, before entering the shrine-room, we exchanged gowns or jackets for robes of plain white cloth with huge winged sleeves. After a month or so I went one better by arriving dressed in Chinese clothes although, in those days, it took real courage for an Englishman to wear 'native dress' in a British colony. It meant being heartily despised by most of one's own countrymen and arousing a good deal of politely concealed amusement among the large numbers of Chinese who supposed that progress lay in blind aping of the militarily powerful Western nations, but I was content with the approbation of Ta-hai and his friends.

Happily uncritical of all that these friends saw fit to teach me and ready to do as they did with the minimum of fuss, I tried my utmost to behave like any other member of the Forest of Recluses, although the others were so accommodating and good-natured as to have freely forgiven any reluctance on my part. For example, aware that most Englishmen thought it demeaning to bow their heads to the ground, they would gladly have absolved me from the obligation to kowtow to Lai Fa-shih as our Dharma-Master; whereas I, anxious to avoid what in Chinese eyes would have been considered impropriety, insisted on kowtowing to him, even though for some reason it did make me blush most laughably. This description of my attitude at that time has its importance in relation to what I now have to say of mantras, the point being that I took every aspect of those elaborate Shingon rites for granted, being moved by their beauty and confident that they must have a deep symbolic meaning that would become apparent in due course. This, I believe, is a surer foundation for gaining real knowledge about such matters than its converse – a preconception that, because something seems trivial or nonsensical in terms of one's own culture, it must necessarily be so. Patiently I learnt how to lace my fingers to form mudras (ritual gestures) and to recite mantras, although at the time I knew no better than to confuse them with magic spells. Besides Ta-hai, two others, feeling a benevolent interest in the young English neophyte, took me specially under their wing – Pun Yin-ta whom the younger members addressed as Elder Brother, and a relative of his who seemed to be universally styled Fifth Uncle. With their help I mastered

just enough of the formal aspect of the rites to be able to participate without too much awkwardness.

On entering the shrine-room we would first stand facing a
window and perform some purificatory mudras, each with its
appropriate mantra which was as resonant to my ear as it was
mystifying to my mind. Then, facing the shrine, we would bow
our heads to the floor thrice before seating ourselves cross-
legged on the cushions. Close to the low altar sat the chief
celebrant (often it was Fifth Uncle), so that the censer and other
ritual implements were comfortably within his reach. To one
side sat the musicians who would accompany the rite with
clarinet, dulcimer (played by Elder Brother), tinkling instruments and a drum. Starting with a melodious incense-chant and
ending with a final mantra, the principal rite lasted rather more
than an hour. Some passages of the liturgy were sung; others,
including the mantras, were chanted or intoned, but in a manner
that bore little resemblance to the chanting that forms parts of
Catholic or Orthodox rituals. The mantras, which were generally recited 3, 7, 21 or 108 times depending partly on their
length, were all couched in the strange language neither Chinese
nor truly Indian of which I have given an example; they were
accompanied by complicated gestures which the others performed with charming grace, whereas my fingers, lacking
Chinese suppleness, betrayed the awkwardness I felt. The
liturgy was so beautiful that, although as yet I understood nothing of its meaning, I gladly put up with the torment of leg-
cramp. Miserably distracting as the pain would otherwise have
been, I sat lost in fascination up to the moment when I had
somehow to struggle to my feet and perform the final triple
prostration.

I wish I could offer a lucid account of the inner significance
of those rites and of what it was that brought to the faces of
the other participants the expression of people undergoing a
profound spiritual experience. Alas, I did not attend the sessions for long enough to reach the point of understanding them
intuitively; and, although my friends did their best to expound
the text of the liturgy, my knowledge of Chinese (or rather of
the Cantonese dialect spoken in Hong Kong) was too rudimen-
tary then for me to make much progress. Fifth Uncle and the

others tried patiently to instruct me in their pleasantly accented English, but the subject matter was difficult, and much of what they did get through to me I have since forgotten owing to my subsequent preoccupation with more purely Chinese (and, later, Tibetan) forms of Buddhism. The main purpose of the rites was to promote mystical intuition of two interpenetrating realms of consciousness, the relative and absolute; the mantras and mudras were part of the means whereby the external rites aroused deep intuitive experience of the mysteries they symbolised.

However, some vague inkling of the power of mantras was conveyed to me by the recitation 108 times of a single syllable – BRONG. At a certain point in the liturgy, the drum would be struck repeatedly and, at each stroke, we would utter a deep-voiced BRONG! What the word means and how it would be pronounced in pure Sanskrit, I do not know, but the effect of participating in its rhythmic recitation was extraordinary. BRONG! BRONG! BRONG! While those 108 cries reverberated, a preternatural stillness fell. My mind, now totally oblivious of the leg pains, soared upwards and entered a state of blissful serenity. This transition, which my consciousness was destined to undergo in greater or in lesser measure in response to other mantras, is something to be understood only from experience; it can never be captured in words. At the time it was so novel and, in a way, so shattering that the return to a normal state of consciousness brought with it something of the terror one would feel on stepping back from the brink of a measureless void! None of the other mantras we recited at those sessions produced a marked effect on me, so I came to attribute the magic not to the mantra but to the drum-beats – a misconception that was not cleared up until many years later.

Whenever I questioned him about the meaning, purpose or operation of mantras, Ta-hai, who spoke scarcely any English, left it to Fifth Uncle to explain. We had already had one conversation on the subject which had gone something like this:

'Uncle, during the *fa* [rite], there are some parts which I think are called *chou* [mantras]. The way of reciting them is so strange and even the language doesn't sound a bit like Chinese. It wouldn't be Japanese, would it?'

Smiling broadly, eyes crinkled with amusement, he thought a moment and then brought out some such outrageous word as 'Hongcanjapchinsanskese' whereat, after looking puzzled for a moment, everyone within hearing burst out laughing.

'What in the world does that mean?' I asked.

'Ha-ha! It mean sounds you hear are Hong Kong Cantonese way of speaking Master Lai's Cantonese-Japanese reading of Chinese words write down thousand years ago so we can know what sounds Indian monks make when use Sanskrit mantras! Maybe ghosts of Indian monks surprised if they come here to listen to us now. Maybe not recognise one word, eh, Ah Jon?'

As it happens, Uncle's little joke embodied an important principle to which I have given much thought while preparing to write this book. It has so often been represented even by knowledgeable people, that a mantra's effectiveness depends on the *vibrations* it arouses and therefore on an exceedingly accurate enunciation. Were that truly so, Sanskrit mantras uttered by Chinese, Tibetans or Japanese could scarcely ever be effective, for the sounds they make are often unrecognisable as Sanskrit! Thus SVĀHĀ in Sanskrit becomes SOHA in Chinese and Tibetan, SAWAKA in Japanese. Similarly AUM becomes OM, UM and even UNG, ONG or ANG in various languages and dialects and yet remains marvellously effective when the mental conditions governing the use of mantric syllables are properly observed. It follows that one must accept the Lama Govinda's assertion to the effect that the real power of mantras resides less in their sound than in the mind of the mantra-wielder. This is undoubtedly wholly true of mantras used in the course of yogic contemplation, although it is just possibly less true of mantras used for certain other purposes.

The next time I spoke to Fifth Uncle on the subject, it was to ask a question which those ignorant of the operation of mantras are apt to ask with a good deal of scorn. 'Uncle, how *can* words that have no meaning even for the person who utters them be of any use at all, let alone assist his spiritual progress? One surely cannot suppose that supernatural agencies respond only to those who address them in a particular language?'

This time he did not smile. Groping for a way of expressing his thought in English, he replied earnestly: 'Words with meaning just good for ordinary use – not much power and get in your way like rocks upsetting a boat. Words with much power not show out real meaning – best forget meaning and keep mind free.'

I doubt if I understood him properly at the time, but now I know that he sought to convey something of the profound mystery that lies at the very heart of the matter. For the time being I had to continue taking the wisdom of my friends' belief in the efficacy of mantras on trust. This I did all the more willingly after chancing to discover that Fifth Uncle, far from relying on blind faith or hearsay, was in his way an expert; by the use of rites involving mantras he had gained an extraordinary victory over one of the most formidable demons known to man! As recounted in detail in my earlier book, *The Wheel of Life*, he had recently cured himself of a life-long addiction to opium involving massive daily doses, without resorting either to medical aid or to the method of gradual withdrawal; renouncing the drug suddenly and completely, he had relied entirely upon the resources of his own mind strengthened by the performance of yogic rites for many hours each day over a period of several months. During all that time he had remained deaf to the appeals of his tearful relatives who assured him that his obstinacy in refusing medical treatment would cost him his life. The dire effects of sudden withdrawal from massive and long-standing use of opiates are now so widely known that Fifth Uncle's feat will be more readily appreciated than when that earlier book first appeared; especially in the case of elderly people those effects, unless mitigated by clinical treatment, generally prove fatal. Scarcely less remarkable is the fact that, despite the shock to his nervous system that must have resulted from an abrupt withdrawal after more than thirty years of indulgence, Uncle completely recovered his health and thereafter remained untroubled by the craving. Once when we were passing the night with a party of friends in a Taoist temple in the mountains of Kwangtung, someone who knew nothing of Uncle's past suggested that we idle away the evening with a little opium, whereupon a tray of implements was brought in, and Uncle spent a couple of hours lying beside the lamp and preparing the pipes with his own hands for one person after another. There he lay smiling benignly as the smoke clouds with their once-seductive aroma rolled above the couch; perfectly at ease as his fingers twirled the silver prong upon which pill after pill of opium was held bubbling above the lamp, he chatted of this and that, serenely unmoved by what for others in his situation must have been a temptation far more excruciating than that suffered by a reformed alcoholic serving at a bar with no one to say him nay!

When, secretly ashamed of allowing him to be put to such a test, we expressed our admiration, he told us laughingly that his private shrine-room had been the best of clinics and the power of mantras the best of medicines!

To return to those earlier conversations about mantras, there came a time when my Western-trained mind balked at accepting the notion that 'meaningless words can be imbued with power'. The more I thought about those passages of the liturgy recited in corrupt Sanskrit, the more I came to feel they must involve a large element of self-delusion. Then, one evening the mantric recitations in the shrine-room left me in a strangely exalted state that could not be wholly attributed to the sensuous spell wrought by the eerie music, sonorous chanting and odour of sandalwood incense. As usual some of us lingered on the veranda after the rite, chatting quietly. Noticing my air of elation, someone remarked approvingly: 'Ah Jon is beginning to find his way.'

The others smiled, but I said: 'I wonder? The rites are intended to help us reach a state in which we gain some perception of the mind's true nature – Mind that is not yours or mine, but the play of the limitless Tao. Just now it seemed to be so, but it may have been just the effect of so much beauty and of being carried away by the serenity of the people all around me.'

Gently they questioned me further and somehow I happened to blurt out the opinion that mantras and mudras could do no more than add a pleasing sense of mystery to the rite. At this an old gentleman, whose name I do not recall (though I have a clear recollection of his gown of shimmering white silk which had not yet taken on the pleasing yellowish tinge that comes with age), said tersely in Cantonese: 'Youngsters must learn to walk before they offer opinions about flying.'

Such a chilling reproof, coming from one who had more than once hinted at the impropriety of admitting a non-initiate to their rites, made it impossible to pursue the matter; but a younger man, sorry to see me so put down, made a point of overtaking me on the way to the nearest tram-stop and persuaded me to 'burn night' (a Cantonese expression meaning take a late-night snack) with him at a nearby teahouse. Over a bowl of noodles, he waxed eloquent on the subject of mantras.

'Ordinary people, Ah Jon, use mantras as spells to win good fortune or ward off disease and other evils. Perhaps they are right to do so, for the mantras are often successful, but I do not ask you to believe that. What I beg you to believe is that they are of the greatest help in altering states of consciousness. They do this by making your mind stay still instead of chasing after thoughts.'

He went on to explain that, being devoid of meaning, they do not promote conceptual thought as prayers, invocations and so forth are apt to do; and that, as each mantra has a mysterious correspondence (he could not explain what kind of correspondence) with the various potentialities embedded deeply in our consciousness (perhaps he meant the subconscious) it could cause one to snap into a state otherwise hard to reach. I do not remember his actual words, but I do know he was the first to voice an idea which was later to be abundantly confirmed by my own experience. That is why I still remember the occasion so vividly. Sitting with me on the upper deck of a tram bound for the centre of Hong Kong, he went on to say that to use meaningful words in any kind of religious practice is useless, since words encourage dualistic thought which hinders the mind from entering upon a truly spiritual state. His last words, delivered rather loudly as I was preparing to disembark from the tram, were: 'People who pray with words are just beginners. Don't do it!' Several passengers who understood English glanced at him as though they thought him a bit mad and I myself was quite taken aback by his un-Chinese vehemence, but I know now that he was eminently sane.

Fifth Uncle's command of English, though very adequate for most purposes, was insufficient for me to be quite sure of how he regarded mantras, but I fancy he too believed that the *sound* of mantric syllables evoked corresponding movements within the depths of the mantra-wielder's consciousness. This emphasis on sound was especially puzzling in the light of his joke about 'Hongcanjapchinsanskese'. I wonder whether he was perhaps referring to a kind of 'ideal sound' – say, a mental concept of the sound OM rather than the particular sound that issues from each individual's lips? Unfortunately Fifth Uncle died many, many years before this question first occurred to me.

A month or so after that memorable tram-ride, I received the first of the two main Shingon initiations, but benefited less than I had hoped; the esoteric manual to which I had now gained access was of course written in Chinese and I could not make very much sense of it even with the help of my English-speaking friends. What is more, my study of Shingon soon ended abruptly owing to my being caught up by Ta-hai's suddenly developed enthusiasm for another branch of esoteric Buddhism – the Vajrayana. This new and fascinating study had much to do with mantras, but again I was balked by the difficulty of the Chinese texts. For some time to come, the only consideration that restrained me from reverting to outright disbelief in the efficacy of mantras was faith in the wisdom of Ta-hai, Fifth Uncle and the others; it would have been presumptuous for a youth reared in a culture alien to their own to dismiss out of hand any of the convictions of men so wise.

Of the Shingon mantras I learnt in those early days, there is one that runs: ONG KALO KALO SENDARI MATONGI SAWAKA. I cannot remember for what purpose it is intended, but it has proved to be peculiarly effective in allaying fear or hysteria in others. If the effect of mantras were limited to power to comfort and heal, they would be spiritually of no greater significance than a white witch's spells; but I know my friends believed that there are mantras and mantras, rising in ascending order from remedies for temporary ills to a misty apex beyond the vision of all but accomplished mystics. Naturally the great mantras were not taught to neophytes – one does not need a bulldozer to crush an ant, or use a toothpick to harpoon a whale!

Shortly before I left Hong Kong for China, an event of great significance to my life – though I did not attach very much importance to it at the time – opened the way to some precious knowledge of yogic contemplation, including mantric practices and much else besides, of which I was to take advantage more than twenty years later. This was my first initiation into the Vajrayana Sect, which has long been the chief repository of the yogic wisdom expounded almost two thousand years ago at India's great monastic university, Nalanda. When Ta-hai rather abruptly began persuading me that it would be best to look beyond Shingon for methods of attaining swift mystical realisation, my studies of the Shingon doctrine of two interpenetrating realms of consciousness, the Garbhadhatu (Relative Realm) and Vajradhatu (Absolute Realm) were halted. My friend's enthusiasm for what (rightly, I think) he held to be the much richer and more widely varied store of yogic knowledge possessed by the lamas of Tibet carried me away, though it caused astonishment and some disapprobation among many of his friends. At that time, the Vajrayana was scarcely known in Hong Kong or in southeast China generally, although it had twice been widely prevalent in the north, once under the Mongol Dynasty (A.D. 1280–1368) and again under the Ta Ch'ing Dynasty established by the Manchus (1644–1911). How far my friend's previous studies had been leading him in that direction I do not know; what brought the matter to a head was the arrival in Hong Kong of a famous Tibetan lama able to teach directly in Chinese, instead of through an (often incompetent) interpreter. Then, as now, this was a rare accomplishment. Yielding to Ta-hai's persuasion, the lama agreed to stay in Hong Kong long enough to instruct a group of Chinese laymen who, being already well-versed in Buddhist doctrine and yogic practice, could soon be made ready for a comprehensive initiation that would empower them to perform the yogas he taught even after his departure for Lhasa. Once again, thanks to Ta-hai's warm-hearted sponsorship, the English youth Ah Jon was accepted into a circle of mystics, although far from qualified for that honour.

Having obtained the lama's permission for me to be admitted, Ta-hai exclaimed excitedly in Cantonese: 'The Shingon teachings brought from Mount Koya by Master Lai, though precious, comprise less than a tithe of what we are about to learn from this Tibetan lama!' But upon this point the members of the Forest of Recluses were divided; some eagerly enrolled for the lama's course of study; others, including Fifth Uncle and Elder Brother, thoughtfully stood aside. The teaching went forward day and night for weeks on end. Handicapped by language problems and by my job – I had begun teaching in a school at the further end of the Kowloon peninsula – I made little progress, in spite of which I was permitted to receive the initiation that formed the culminating point of our studies. Just as Ta-hai had been moved by happiness on encountering a Western Buddhist (a rare species in the China of those days), so it was with the lama. Each in turn accorded me unheard of privileges. The lama, brushing aside my modest protests with a smile, remarked that, although it might be years before I could make much use of the initiation, he had 'sown some seeds' in my mind that could be relied upon to blossom at the proper season.

The importance of that initiation in the present context is that, besides opening the way for me to study the Vajrayana in the years to come, it prevented me from yielding to growing scepticism regarding mantras, for the lama was very persuasive on that subject. Even so, though I dutifully memorised the Tibeto-Sanskrit mantras required for the initiation, I could summon up little more than a wistful half-belief in their power over mind. Soon after the lama's departure, I left for the Chinese mainland where I wandered for many years, taking up teaching posts when acutely short of money, often staying for weeks or months at a time in Buddhist or Taoist monasteries, and every now and then returning to Hong Kong to visit my dear friends.

Alas, it is years since Fifth Uncle, Ta-hai and Elder Brother passed away in turn. Though it is to Ta-hai especially that I owe the abiding interest of my later years, Vajrayana yogic contemplation, my debt to them all is immense. It would please me to know that my writings on Chinese and Tibetan Buddhism represent a not altogether unworthy flowering of the teaching which, accompanied by many other kindnesses, they showered upon Ah Jon, an English youth who came to them empty-handed.

Chapter 2

The Lost Tradition

Gone now were the evenings passed among white-robed figures bathed in golden light, rapturously intoning the mantric syllable BRONG. I had entered another, but not very dissimilar, world where my companions were Chinese monks, black-robed, shaven-headed. It was the hour before dawn and the scene was a great temple hall with double-tiered, curving roofs rising amidst the flower-decked courtyards of a monastery. Upon the high altar innumerable candles blazed, brilliantly illumining three tall, gilded statues – the Buddhas of the Triple World; yet the hall with its gorgeously painted pillars and roof-beams was sombre; it was too vast for the light to do more than pick out the faces of the throng of worshippers. Their dark monastic robes merged with the surrounding gloom so that, at times, the sea of pale faces resembled those of disembodied spirits. Hitherto these monks had been ranged before the altar, but they had turned and now stood in serried rows forming two groups which faced each other across a central aisle running from the altar to the massive doorway. Standing among the group to the right, I was able to observe the expressions of those to the left. On my side, the precentor, wielding a mallet shaped like a lotus bud rising from its stem, was beating out a mantric rhythm on the 'wooden-fish drum', a huge rounded block of wood so called on account of some fancied resemblance to a fish's head; and now and then another monk punctuated the chanting by striking a great bronze sounding-bowl. To this sonorous accompaniment, the assembly was intoning a long mantra couched in a language no longer recognisable as Sanskrit; but, as I now knew, its effect depended not at all upon the conceptual meaning of the sacred syllables. The wave of sound was certainly uplifting; as the notes welled forth, my mind was borne aloft on wings of no-thought by the power of an ancient mystery and I longed to add my voice to the others.

In such surroundings it would have been pardonable to suppose that the age-old mantric tradition still flourished. It was not so. Fortunately for me, an interest in mantras was not among the reasons that had led to my preparing to make a long stay in that monastery. I had come to China in search of whatever venerable ways of life survived the onslaught of innovations from the strident West and I was eager to acquire something of value to my spiritual development; mantras, for all their fascination, were essential to neither of those quests, so I was not cast down by the discovery that only remnants of the ancient mantric tradition still lingered in China, probably because the Esoteric Sect (Mi Tsung) from which knowledge of mantras had formerly been derived had long been moribund. Mantras, though still prominent in the monastic liturgy which had remained unchanged for centuries, were now esteemed as a means of wooing good fortune and as magic spells rather than as aids to spiritual development. The following is one of the innumerable stories I heard which served to reinforce this conviction.

One evening soon after my arrival at the monastery, I was strolling through the surrounding woods with Su Ting, a young monk who had made himself my mentor and companion. By chance he had spoken of the power of mantras and, finding me somewhat sceptical, he said warmly:

'Are all Western Ocean people as hard to convince as you? How strange! You have only to use your eyes and ears a little to discover such things for yourselves. You recall Hui Ting, the monk to whom you gave those biscuits when he set out with the other pilgrims for the Golden Pagoda in Burma? He could have told you. Some years ago when he was still a schoolboy in his native city, Mengtsê, he was friendly with a merchant's son surnamed Kao. When he finally decided to "leave home" (become a monk), Kao thought him crazy and shouted to the neighbours not to let a promising youth throw away his happiness for "a lot of superstitious nonsense". You know how people are. After that they naturally lost sight of each other for several years. Hui Ting, having taken his vows, came to join us here five or six years ago. Then, last winter, someone came banging on the monastery gate long after dark. On being admitted, he brusquely demanded that the Receiver of Guests take him at once to see "young Chang from Mengtsê". Chang is such a common surname and of course we who have left home never use surnames anyway, so it took a little time to discover he meant Hui Ting. Our visitor, as you must have guessed, was Kao. As soon as the two of them were alone together, Hui Ting remarked:

'"You have changed, old friend. I cannot say I see you look-ing well. You have grown thin. As for your complexion, your cheeks used to be as ruddy as the War God's and now—"

'"You are right, little shaven-pate. What else should bring me to this lair of misguided eunuchs? I've been ill. Doctors are no help and so, as a last resort, I've come to you just in case there's something in your sacred nonsense. You used to have a good deal of sense, which forces me to suppose you must have had a good reason for being so eager to renounce the joys of the world. As a boy you had an eye for pretty girls; now, you cannot even take a wife, let alone play around with charm-ing little wenches skilled in music and you-know-what."

'Hui Ting smiled. Remembering it was old Kao himself who had been taken up with courtesans, he was not in the least affronted at this way of putting things. "Never mind my troubles—they are not what you suppose. What has brought you banging on our gate at this time of a freezing winter's night?"

'Kao's story was that, a year or two ago, he had driven his wife all too abruptly into the world of ghosts. Forever harping on his infidelities, she had goaded him into striking her and, stumbling backwards from the blow, had cracked her head against the corner of a heavy table. The injury, aggravated by the virulent poison of hatred, had presently caused her death. Nor was that all. No sooner was she in her coffin than he began to suffer from violent pains in the part of his head exactly corres-ponding to her fatal injury.

'"Her spirit's reaching for me", moaned Kao. "I cannot work. I cannot rest. I've given up my shop and the price I got for it has been swallowed up by a pack of incompetent physicians. Now they say I have an incurable tumour. Unless Your Reverence can suggest a cure for it, I'm done for. Death in itself would not be too bad, but imagine having to face that malevolent ghost in the spirit world!''

'Being no doctor, Hui Ting was at sevens and eights. He wanted to help, but how? His only skill lies in meditation. All he could think of was to form a powerful aspiration for his friend's well-being and invoke the Healing Buddha. This proved unexpectedly effective. Passing into a state of stillness, he presently opened his eyes and, as he did so, heard a voice coming from his lips which said: "Go back to Mengtsê. Get up before dawn each day. Wrap yourself against the cold and go to sit by the pool in the compound of the Temple of the Compassionate Kuan Yin in the eastern precinct of the city. Keeping your gaze upon the water, recite the mantra I shall teach you some thousands of times each morning. The first signs of success will be the appearance of ripples upon the water as though a stone had been cast therein and a lessening of your pain. If you concentrate rightly, these ripples, aroused by your mind, will become more pronounced each day. Continue thus until the Merciful One manifests herself by rising from the centre of the concentric ripples. When that happens, salute her humbly and depart. There will be no need to go again."

'Kao did as the voice had commanded. Within a few days his pain grew less intense and, although he once caught cold from sitting patiently by the pool during a light snowstorm, he persisted until the mantric syllables, proceeding effortlessly from his mind, caused circular ripples as predicted. On the fifteenth day of the second moon, he saw a white fish leap from amidst the ripples and, remaining in the air for the space of three gong-strokes, manifest itself as a radiant figure clad in head-dress and robes of pure white, though not larger than a new-born infant. Bowing to the earth three times, Kao ran joyfully home. The cure was complete and now, every year, he comes here on the Compassionate Kuan Yin's Birthday to take part in the celebrations and make offerings to our fraternity.'

Su Ting assured me that the ripples on the lake and the appearance of the Compassionate Bodhisattva in miniature form were objective phenomena evoked by the mantra in conjunction with the powerful concentration of Kao's mind. Though unconvinced, I did not wholly reject the possibility of Su Ting's being right. Now I am sure he was, for mantras pronounced with deep sincerity unlock creative mental powers of which we are not normally aware. Even so, the story exemplifies Chinese preoccupation with an aspect of mantras that is of but secondary importance.

Stories of this kind naturally made me doubly curious about the mantras that formed part of the monastic liturgy used throughout China, regardless of whether a particular monastery happened to be of the Ch'an (Zen) Sect, the Ching T'u (Pure Land) Sect or any other. It proved hard to obtain much information on the subject. The senior monks to whom I went for guidance generally turned aside my questions by expatiating on the excellence of certain devotional formulas which, though not unlike mantras in effect, belonged to a different category of sacred utterance, as will be seen. Whereas mantras are called *chou* in Chinese, the devotional formulas are known as *nien-fu* (which corresponds to the Sanskrit *japa*). Both induce a contemplative state of mind that is free from dualistic thought, but outwardly they differ widely; for, whereas mantras arouse a response directly within the devotee's own mind, *nien-fu* formulas are ostensibly appeals for a divine response from without. However, this difference holds good only at the level of relative truth, there being no division in the ultimate sense between inside and outside in such matters, for our minds and Mind are recognised by all accomplished yogins to be one. Indeed the highest purpose of yogic endeavour is to achieve a direct experience of the unity of minds and Mind; though Christian and Sufi mystics conceive of this experience as *attaining* union between man and God, and though Buddhist and Taoist adepts think of it as *realising* a state of union with the Ultimate Source which, from the first, has never ceased to be, these are but conceptual differences with no ultimate validity. Within the fold of Buddhism, the use of *nien-fu* formulas very superficially resembles a theistic approach, whereas the other approaches, including that

in which mantras are used, are more obviously free from theism; yet in essence and in result they are the same. An account
of the liturgical use of both mantras and *nien-fu* formulas follows.

Daily before sunrise the community in every Chinese Buddhist monastery was summoned to the shrine-hall by the resonant
clang of a gong-like sheet of bronze alternating with the thunder
of a gigantic drum. Assembling before the gleaming statues of
the Buddhas of the Triple World, which were sometimes so
lofty that the carven features and enigmatic smiles betokening
mind-born bliss were lost in shadow, the monks would thrice
prostrate themselves, their movements governed by the notes
of a silver chime. Then would arise a solemn incense hymn as
a prelude to rites wherein three main strands were woven:
chants of blessing and aspiration (the closest Buddhist equivalent to prayer); the recitation of mantras; and the utterance
of devotional (*nien-fu*) formulas addressed to Amitabha, embodiment of wisdom's light, or to Avalokitesvara (Kuan Yin),
embodiment of supreme compassion. One truly formidable
mantra composed of some three thousand syllables took close
on thirty minutes to recite, though the rhythm beaten out upon
the wooden-fish drum was brisk rather than slow. Such liturgical mantras were uttered in a manner too monotonous to be
called song and yet more tuneful and varied than what can properly be called chanting; though it must have originated in India,
the tune was no longer recognisable as Indian. Every monk
could recite the entire liturgy by heart, and, although the
mantric sections contained no intelligible meaning, I could see
from the expressions of those standing across the aisle that they
inspired rapture. True, there were always a handful of monks
suffering from coughs or colds and some fidgety young novices
who looked as if they were longing for the rite to end, but most
of the assembly stood motionless, eyes half closed and bliss
lit large upon their faces. I, too, felt invaded and uplifted by
that stream of solemn sound, wishing I could take part.
Daunted by the difficulty of memorising it, I never learnt the
longest of the mantras; but most of the others I managed to
commit to memory, including the 415-syllable Ta Pei Chou
(Mantra of Great Compassion) which, upon certain occasions,

was repeated twenty-one or even a hundred-and-eight times in succession.

There was one old monk who, in response to my question about the source of the calm serenity inspired by mantras, replied that it was their *sound* which in some mysterious way enabled the mind to grasp its hidden affinity with the Tao, the Source of Being, but the answer struck me as too vague. I was still inclined then to suppose that the effect was akin to hypnosis and owed more to the rhythm of the wooden-fish drum and the melodious clang of the great bronze sounding-bowl than to the mantras themselves; even so, I was able to recognise the superiority of mantric utterance to prayer, for prayers convey a conceptual meaning and by evoking thought mar the stillness of the adept's mind. One's mind cannot attain a calm, untroubled state reflecting the serenity of the Source for as long as it dwells on such dualisms as 'I, the worshipper; He, the worshipped'. Prayer is at best an elementary form of mystical communion; as for prayers that contain petitions, what can be more unspiritual and self-seeking than to pray for victory, a particular state of weather or good fortune that can be attained only at the expense of others? That I still confused the operation of mantras with something akin to hypnotic power was not surprising. Westerners trained to question, analyse, investigate, are thereby hindered from spontaneously achieving mystical ecstasy.

As to the other components of the Chinese Buddhist liturgy, by far the most interesting was the recitation of devotional formulas – *nien-fu* practice; although I also enjoyed the chants of blessing and aspiration on account of the richness of their imagery. Such images as 'Buddha Shining with Golden Flower Light', 'Buddha Gleaming with the Pearly Radiance of Sun and Moon' do perhaps promote intuitive realisation of the mystical experience, which is generally accompanied by perception of inner light.

Namo O-mi-to Fu (Reverence to Amitabha Buddha or to the Embodiment of Boundless Light), the most widely used *nien-fu* formula, has, of course, a conceptual meaning, but it was used in the manner in which mystics of the Orthodox Church employ the Jesus Prayer, that is to say as a means of transcending conceptual thought and establishing communion with That Which Lies Within. Recitation of the formula constituted an important part of the evening rite. The monks, whether they numbered a handful or several hundred, would perambulate the shrine-hall in single file, sometimes gliding behind the gilded statues, sometimes threading in and out of the space between the statues and the altar whereon lamps and candles blazed. At the head walked the abbot or chief celebrant, followed by the precentor, who beat out the rhythm upon a portable wooden-fish drum decorated with gold and scarlet lacquer. Initially the pace was slow and the voices lingered upon each syllable – NA-a-a-a MO-o-o-o-o O-a-a-a-a MI-a-a-a-a- TO-a-a-a- FU-u-u-a-a-a. Presently the tempo would quicken, the cloth-soled shoes fall faster and the invocation take on a growing urgency. Towards the end, the monks moved forward as fast as could be without actually breaking into a shuffling run, whereat the invocation would be shortened to four swiftly uttered syllables – Omito Fu, Omito Fu, Omito Fu. ... Then, as fervour rose and voices soared to a crescendo, a bell-like note struck from the sounding-bowl which would bring the procession to a halt. There would come a moment's silence, broken perhaps by a sigh. Then, CLANG! At this further signal from the great bronze sounding-bowl, the monks would decorously hurry back to their places in the body of the hall for the concluding stages of the rite.

Exoterically, they had been calling upon Amitabha Buddha to admit them at death to his Pure Land where, freed from all mundane obstacles, they could prepare themselves for the ineffable bliss of Nirvana. Esoterically, the Pure Land was recognised as something to be attained within the devotee's own mind – a state of stillness that would supervene when the mind was purged of inordinate desire and illumined by compassion, a perfect unity of minds and Mind! It was taught that recital of the holy name with perfect concentration a thousand times, ten thousand times a day, whether with mind and lips or with mind alone, and regardless of what slight attention must be given to the business of the day, would promote attainment of a holy state beyond conceptual thought. The consciousness, freed from crippling distinctions between thinker and thinking,

thinking and object of thought, would expand and take on the vastness and sublimity of the Ultimate Source – Amitabha recognised as Pure Mind, the Tao, Nirvana!

Naturally I was ignorant of the inner meaning of the Pure Land doctrine in those early days; the monks in their wisdom refrained from expounding such subtle doctrines to novices and I had no Ta-hai or Fifth Uncle to whisper short-cuts to understanding into my ear. It is best, moreover, to leave such life-giving knowledge to dawn of itself. Nevertheless I had already managed to grasp that the *nien-fu* practice followed during the evening rite was not essentially different from the morning practice of reciting mantras; both involved the use of words in a manner that transcended meaning.

Having dreamt of China from afar since soon after reaching my eleventh year, I was eager to see more and more of what was for me a magic land. My restless journeying took me to innumerable Buddhist and Taoist sanctuaries, some of them large monasteries, others small and rarely visited temples. The sites had been chosen with a loving regard for nature's charms. One would come upon curving roofs tiled with green, blue or yellow porcelain rising like those of a fairy palace from amidst groves of cedar or clumps of feathery bamboo. Sometimes their crimson or magenta walls could be seen clinging to a rocky ledge perched high above a foaming torrent, or an elegant pagoda be discerned upon the crest of a lakeside eminence, its eleven or thirteen storeys mirrored on the surface of the water. Beauty upon beauty! The imposing gateways of these sanctuaries formed the threshold to a world of mystery. The very kitchens and washrooms, even the sheds concealing the latrine-pits, would have upon some wall or pillar a slip of scarlet paper inscribed with a mantra appropriate to cooking, washing or emptying one's bowels, precious reminders of the sanctity of every action, every object, not excluding that which fills the undiscerning with disgust. Thus the monks were exhorted to make no less use of the time spent on chores and ablutions than of the hours they passed in the meditation hall. Complete negation of the ego, conscious union with the Source of Being is a task so hard to accomplish within one lifetime that not a moment may be wasted; for, if the opportunity is missed, who knows how many lifetimes must elapse before the conditions needed for further progress are encountered? Such at least were the thoughts that had originally inspired the posting up of mantras in such unlikely places, but long familiarity had dulled their message. It is doubtful whether as many as one monk in ten or twenty actually recited a mantra as he squatted above the cesspit.

I regret now having failed to inquire why certain mantras in particular were deemed appropriate to ablution or defecation. The answer might have shed some light on the question as to why a whole series of *different* mantras are needed to suit varieties of circumstance, whereas one *nien-fu* formula is thought entirely sufficient for use in all contingencies.

There were special mantras for use at meal-times. The monks, having entered the refectory, would stand in silence while one of their number made an offering to the wandering spirits believed to throng invisibly about us. Lifting a few grains of rice with his chopsticks, he would lay them upon a squat stone pillar graven in the form of a lotus that stood in the adjoining courtyard. So doing, he would recite a mantra and mentally convert the offering into a great feast. Though unconvinced then of the existence of those invisible throngs, I admired the practice, taking it as a daily reminder of the Buddhist duty of compassion to every kind of sentient being and of the yogic truth that nothing is ever what it seems, the apparent solidity of objects being illusory, visible and invisible being equally real or unreal.

Most beautiful and mysterious of all the monastic rites was the one used to appease the hunger of the 'fiery-mouths' or tantalised spirits of once avaricious men. When a death occurred, it was the custom for the relatives of the deceased to perform various charitable acts wherewith to build up his stock of merit and thus exercise a benign influence on the conditions of his next existence; these generally included the free distribution of some such sacred text as the Diamond Sutra and the holding of a banquet for the fiery-mouths. For this rite, the chief officiant, clad in a robe of crimson and gold and wearing the five-petalled lotus hat of a Bodhisattva, would sit at the head of a long narrow table with his assistants ranged on stools to either side and equipped with such accessories as liturgical books, drums, bells and ritual implements. The table was so placed that he faced a courtyard spacious enough to accommodate the host of invisible guests – fiery-mouths with gullets thin as stalks of grass and monstrous pot-bellies who had but to take a grain of rice or sip of water for it to turn immediately into searing flame, unless this sustenance was ritually transformed into *amrta* (nectar) for their comfort.

As the rite proceeded, the officiant's fingers would flutter through a series of mudras as graceful as the gestures of an Indian dancer; meanwhile he would intone a stream of mantric syllables punctuated by the tapping of a wooden-fish drum and the tinkle of a ritual bell. True adepts at this task could produce waves of thrillingly melodious sound. Words cannot portray either the beauty of this rite or the melancholy and awe it kindled in the hearts of the bystanders. The lovely gestures and eerie song with its antique cadences so worked upon the senses that it was easy to visualise the throng of tormented spirits and, as it were, 'hear' their doleful cries as they waited in agonised suspense for the *amtra* that would appease their thirst and hunger. One did not have to believe firmly in those invisible presences to be moved by the drama of the rite, for the world abounds with hungry and destitute beings – human, animal and perhaps members of invisible orders – direly in need of the compassion that blossoms in the mind as yogic experience unfolds.

Striking as were these survivals of a once rich mantric tradition, I was soon forced to the conclusion that real knowledge about the nature and function of mantras had become rare in China, except in the Mongolian and Tibetan border regions where the Vajrayana flourished and in certain cities where it had been re-introduced among small groups of devotees. The prevalence of mantras in the monastic liturgy followed by the Ch'an (Zen) and Pure Land Sects alike was a curious and perhaps fortuitous survival from the days when the defunct Esoteric Sect had flourished. Probably the liturgy had been devised in a form acceptable to all sects at a time when the Esoteric Sect still held its own among the others, the idea being that all approaches to yogic wisdom should be encouraged. Chinese monasteries being strongholds of tradition, no one had thought to revise the liturgy, but it was rare to meet a monk able to expound mantric lore. Having lost sight of the sublimer aspects, most monks were content to regard mantras in the light of magic spells, useful for alleviating illness and transforming offerings to spirits, but of no direct concern to those engaged in the supreme task of attaining mystical realisation. For every Dharma-Master prepared to discourse even briefly on mantras, there were scores who preferred to talk about the marvellous fruits of *nien-fu* practice or of Ch'an contemplative methods. The serenity experienced during the recitation of the liturgical mantras was real enough, yet I feel sure that they had been retained more out of respect for tradition than because careful thought was still given to their value as aids to yogic progress.

Naturally I was a good deal influenced by the ideas of my Chinese teachers and the monks with whom I used to spend weeks or months at a time, so I came to share their attitude to mantras and continued to attribute their effect on me to the sonorous rhythmic chanting rather than to the power of the mantric syllables themselves. But whenever I allowed it to be seen that I took the rites for feeding spirits and fiery-mouths as charming allegories intended to develop spontaneous compassion, the monks would chide my unbelief and ply me with what they certainly believed to be true accounts of the wonders wrought by mantras. Among these stories was one that made a lasting impression on me because, whether true or not, it seemed to hint at what might be the real source of mantric power, if indeed such power existed. I do not remember the name of the Dharma-Master who was the chief protagonist, but I shall call him Hung Kuang Fa-Shih. The story ran as follows:

Dharma-Master Hung Kuang was so marvellously adept at performing rites for the benefit of fiery-mouths and wandering spirits that bystanders would actually behold a throng of ghostly beings pressing about the table where, robed as a Bodhisattva, he sat melodiously intoning the sacred words, hands flying, fingers twirling as the mudras merged one into another. More than once he had been heard to say: 'Among the denizens of all the universes of the ten directions there are none so evil as to have forfeited the Buddha's immeasurable compassion. Those of you who fear for the well-being of your departed kins-folk may whisper their names to me. Though they be guilty of such unspeakable crimes as slaying and eating the flesh of their parents, I shall not fail them. Thus have I vowed before the face of the Compassionate Buddha.' Even the offspring of devils may be moved by filial piety and so it came about that the sons and daughters of decapitated criminals and of other wretches who had died steeped in wickedness would come to this Dharma-Master in secret and implore his aid. Never did he withhold it. One night he admitted to his hermitage a youth who had come to plead for his father, a notorious bandit guilty of not just one but *two* of the five crimes which, according to orthodox Buddhist teaching, are unutterably atrocious. Lead-ing a raid upon a secluded convent, he had joined his comrades in raping and murdering the chaste nuns *and* in 'drawing blood from the body of a Buddha', that is, hacking with their swords at the sacred images!

Sighing at the thought of such senseless and appalling evil, Hung Kuang Fa-Shih assented to the young man's plea and, arousing his closest disciple, made ready there and then to struggle for the release of the tormented spirit. During the rite, the others noticed with concern that now and then the Dharma-Master faltered, cheeks ashy white, hands shaking, voice falling almost to a whisper; but each time he seemed to take heart and the rite proceeded. Emerging from the surrounding darkness, the spirit of the bandit chief appeared. There he stood, bowed beneath a crushing load of guilt. It was easy to mark the joyous moment when the load abruptly fell away. Immediately this shadowy form stood erect and, glaring at the youth, cried in the blood-chilling tones of those who have passed beyond death's threshold: 'Wretched boy! You would have done better to let your father suffer an eon of torment than deprive the world of this holy monk who has saved untold numbers of miserable creatures from a gloomy fate and had many years of life before him!' With these words the spirit vanished. The Dharma-Master, battling against weakness, summoned just enough strength to bring the rite to a close before falling back dead into the arms of his weeping disciple.

At last, turning to the terrified youth, this monk said sorrowfully: 'Our Master was able to release countless spirits by the power of his merit. Every mantra he uttered, each of his sacred gestures, was empowered by the vitality of his steadfast mind. Undoubtedly he knew that to release a spirit burdened with such grievous crimes as your father's would exhaust his entire stock of vital power. Yet, sooner than go back upon his vow, he helped you gladly, though foreseeing that it would cost his life! The least you can do is hasten to enter the monkhood and spend your years acquiring merit wherewith to help a few unhappy spirits in their turn.' This the boy did, but it was poor recompense for such an irreparable loss.

There is another story that lingers in my memory, probably because, whether it is true or originated merely as a moral tale, it contains an element of factuality regarding the nature of mantras. In the province of Honan dwelt two small children, Lao San and Lao Szê. Like Confucius in ancient times, this brother and sister loved to imitate adult ceremonies. Besides performing 'marriages', 'funerals' and 'full-month ceremonies' using dolls to represent the month-old babies, they often visited a usually deserted temple to bow to the ground before the Compassionate Buddha. One day, to their considerable but not really immense surprise, the statue of the Buddha spoke to them, imparting a brief sacred formula whose syllables they carefully memorised, though unable to discern their meaning. This was a secret they kept from others and, whenever some childish trouble loomed, they would repeat the syllables under their breath whereat, or very soon afterwards, the trouble would be averted.

The following winter they chanced to stop by a frozen pond to watch some older children skating. Presently a lad of about fourteen went skimming across the ice to a place nearer the centre of the pond than any of his companions. All of a sudden, with a sound like a gun-shot, the ice cracked and started to give way. Quick as thought, the brother and sister pronounced their sacred formula, whereupon the cracked ice through which the water was welling up held until the skater had reached firmer ice near the shore. Dancing with excitement, Lao San and Lao Szê yelled at the top of their lungs that the big boy owed his life to their magic words. Half-impressed, half-scornful, the other children gathered round demanding an explanation.

'What magic words?' cried one, twisting Lao San's arm till he screamed for mercy. Instinctively the brother and sister knew what would happen if they revealed their secret, but the pain was too great for a little boy to bear. Sobbing bitterly, he blurted out the sacred formula. Naturally the other children demanded a demonstration before setting their victims free. Alas, when applied to saving a stray dog from a volley of well-aimed stones, the mantra failed. Nor did it ever work for Lao San and Lao Szê again.

The truth enshrined in this little story is that adepts of the mantric art who boast of their accomplishment or seek to demonstrate it to others forfeit their power. That is most unfortunate, for recognition of this fact reinforces the natural modesty that comes with spiritual attainment, with the result that one can rarely witness, unless by chance, convincing demonstrations of mantric power. Conviction is usually attainable only as a result of the power that arises within oneself.

That genuine mantric knowledge had at one time been current in China is borne out by several passages in the Buddhist liturgy. For example, there is a passage known as 'Mêng-Shan Shih Shih-I' (literally, 'Bestowal of the Hidden Mount of Offerings') which superficially resembles magic in that the officiant traces with his finger-tip a mantric syllable over a bowl of pure water in order to convert it into *amrta* or, as the Chinese say, *kan-lu* (sweet dew); but it is notable that, just before the mantra, come the words: 'Whosoever desires to comprehend the Buddhas of the Triple World must understand that this whole universe consists of nought but mind.' This, as I came to know years later, is the context in which the whole science of mantras must be understood. In this passage we have a remnant of the profound knowledge formerly transmitted by the Esoteric Sect. Why did that sect, with its fascinating secrets, disappear from China almost a thousand years ago? Probably it employed the sexual imagery which, for perfectly respectable reasons, characterises the Vajrayana Sect of Tibet. If so, the Confucian authorities, ignorant of the exalted nature of the doctrines clothed by that imagery, must certainly have been appalled. The Confucians, without being stern puritans, were shockingly prudish and may well have given orders for the sacred images and paintings to be obliterated. Another possibility is that, awed by reports of the initiates' strange powers, the Confucians mistook them for sorcerers and rigorously suppressed them. Throughout history and in many parts of the world, the charge of witchcraft has all too frequently been levelled at exponents of the more esoteric forms of religion, despite conduct that has usually been blameless and governed by intentions of unblemished purity.

Chapter 3

The Beginning of Understanding

Once more the curtain had risen upon an unfamiliar scene. The great temples I had visited in China lay a thousand miles to the east. Here in the Himalayan foot-hills rising astride the Indo-Tibetan frontier, there were plenty of yogic adepts but no architectural wonders surviving from a bygone age. After some days of walking through the mountains, I had come upon a rustic temple built of materials lying close to hand. Square in shape, it had no pretensions to artistic merit; only a painted doorway and a pyramidal roof proclaimed its sacred purpose. Within the dim interior, a handful of lamas clad in robes of drab maroon sat cross-legged on their floor-cushions facing an altar furnished with butter-lamps, silver bowls of offerings and some of those curious figures called *torma* which are fashioned of buttered dough. Heavy clouds of incense smoke hung upon the air. Where in a richer temple a splendid image might have stood, hung a tattered *thanka* (wall-scroll) depicting a female deity of ferocious aspect, one foot raised and resting upon her knee, the other trampling a solar disc supported by a corpse which lay supine upon a likeness of the moon covering a giant lotus. The diadem girding her flame-like hair was composed of human skulls; a necklace of severed heads adorned her naked, richly crimson flesh. Despite the weirdness of these attributes, I experienced no misgiving, for the expressions of the lamas were reassuringly sweet and gentle; however bizarre the symbols on which they chose to meditate, one could hardly doubt that they were men of kindly disposition and wholesome thoughts. To the eerie tinkle of vajra-bells and the throb of twirling hand-drums struck by pellets attached by leather thongs, they were pouring forth a flood of sound that seemed to rise rather from their bellies than from their vocal organs. More than ever before, I recognised the power of mantras to transport the mind to a state of blissful tranquillity. Also I revelled in the thought that the scene was in every respect like those beheld by travellers in that region a thousand years ago and more.

Before I left China, the seeds implanted in my mind by the Tibetan lama in Hong Kong had been watered now and then, for I had often stayed in Tibetan-style monasteries in the remoter provinces; but it was not until after 1948, the year in which I had sadly bade adieu to the country I loved so well, that I established close contact with Tibetan lamas and began to gain a real insight into the magic world of the Vajrayana. In the decade or so that followed, I paid several protracted visits to the Himalayan foot-hills – to lovely Gangtok and the torrent-girt mountain monastery of Tashiding in Sikkim and to those hill-towns within the borders of India to which so many out-standing lamas had fled during or after the Chinese advance on Lhasa.

Tibetans are in many ways a thoroughly down-to-earth people; in others they are like beings from another age, so rich their satisfaction in simple things, so spontaneous their laughter and so abiding their joy and faith in Chö – the Sacred Dharma. Though, as impoverished exiles, they were often shabbily dressed and lacked the colourful paraphernalia that had lent splendour to their ancient rituals, their rites remained inspir-ing – the roll and clash of cymbals, the elemental power of the sacred melody, the thrilling rhythms of the chants and the enraptured expressions that played upon the faces of the cele-brants. One could see that their minds had soared into a timeless realm full of joy and mystery. Presently I gained a new insight into the nature of mantras; as manifestations of *shabda* (sacred sound), they have qualities in common with Tibetan religious music, which in turn echoes the voice of the wind in high places, the roar of mountain torrents and the crash of thunder.

Some of the treasures of mind to be discovered in the awe-inspiring Himalayan region have been described in three of my earlier books (*The Wheel of Life*, *The Way of Power* and *Beyond the Gods*, George Allen & Unwin); here I shall write particularly of what pertains to mantras. By chance more than by design, the teachings and initiations I received were bestowed mostly by Nyingmapas, that is to say adherents of an ancient sect that flourishes in the eastern marches – Kham and Amdo (Ch'inghai) and in the tiny Himalayan kingdom of Sikkim. There are Buddhists who feel that this 'unreformed' sect errs in having lost much of its monastic character and it is true that Nyingmapa lamas are more often married laymen than monks. Possibly that is to be deplored; nevertheless it is just because the sect escaped 'reformation' that it has been able to preserve without break certain secret traditions extending back to remote antiquity. There being no Buddhist counterpart of the antagonisms and rivalries that so tragically rent Christendom, where the Tibetan sects diverge it is with regard to method rather than doctrine; thus Nyingmapa lamas teach yogic contemplation and exercises at a comparatively early stage, whereas the Gelugpa lamas require of neophytes a long preliminary study of doctrine, with the result that yogic practice has often to be postponed until middle age. Which is the sounder system is a matter of opinion; but my encountering Nyingmapa teachers was certainly an advantage in that they willingly imparted yogic teaching.

By no means all Tibetans are masters of the secret yogic arts. On the contrary, Buddhism flourishes among them at the popular as well as the higher level, so much of what I saw in the beginning was reminiscent of the situation in China where little distinction was made between mantras and magic spells. For example, wherever I went in those mountains, I came upon evidence of prodigious faith in the efficacy of the mantra OM MAŇI PADME HŪM as a protective charm; it was inscribed upon wayside rocks and upon walls specially erected to display it, often with each syllable depicted in its appropriate yogic colour. Everywhere one saw people spinning prayer-mills containing rolls of silk or paper whereon the mantra had been written a hundred or a thousand times; I have heard of larger prayer-mills driven by turbid streams and seen ponderous metal prayer-drums ranged about the gates of temples where every passing pilgrim can cause them to revolve. While twirling their prayer-mills, the devotees intone the mantric syllables and visualise them, too, so that man's three faculties of body, speech and mind are all engaged by – OM MAŅI PADME HŪM! Passengers on long-distance buses, farmers working in the fields and tattered refugees gazing wistfully at shop-windows recite this mantra for hours on end.

Known as the Mani, it is the mantra of the Supremely Compassionate Avalokiteshvara Bodhisattva, who takes the form of Lord Chenresig in Mongolia and Tibet, and of the lovely Kuan Yin (Kannon) in China (and Japan). That Avalokiteshvara is known by the wise not as a god or goddess, but as the mind's embodiment of a force too abstract to be otherwise depicted neither adds to nor detracts from the mantra's power. What to the uninstructed is a beloved deity is, to all alike, a very potent source of inspiration; for Avalokiteshvara, whether regarded as a self-existing celestial being or as a mental creation of the devotee, personifies the tremendous force of compassion impartially bestowed on all sentient beings alike. Nor is the difference in sex between the two manifestations significant, for the sexual attributes of Bodhisattvas are wholly matters of convention. It seems appropriate to embody the spirit of compassion in female form, but the male embodiment, Chenresig, is depicted as a no less gentle-looking being whose sex is obvious only to those familiar with Indo-Tibetan iconographic conventions.

Of the innumerable tales associated with the Mani, my favourite happens to be Chinese, but it is very similar to those current among Tibetans.

A petty warlord noted for ruthless cruelty, having watched his troops leave the field in headlong flight, had to flee himself from his rival's clutches. Having flung off his uniform and donned a peasant's coarse blue homespun, he rode hell for leather into the mountains. Hungry and tired, he pressed forward as fast as his weary horse could carry him. By the second evening he felt secure enough to pass the night at a wayside hermitage. Perceiving that the only inhabitants were an aged Mongolian lama and a young serving-boy, he behaved with brutal truculence, forcing them to pack his empty saddle-bags with such portable valuables as the hermitage contained. Purloining his hosts' possessions was after all his customary manner of repaying hospitality, since the sole function of civilians was to enable heroes to live well. The monks' cells being small and comfortless, he ordered them to place a couch for him in the shrine-hall and there, undisturbed by the light of two votive candles illumining a statue of the Compassionate Kuan Yin, he fell into a fitful sleep. Sorry for his boorish persecutor, the old lama presently crept close to the couch and, sitting cross-legged on the flagstones in a shadowed place, set himself to repeating the mantra OM MAŅI PADME HŪM, which he continued to do in a low hum all through the night; except that, whenever he saw the warlord stir in his sleep, he formed the syllables silently with his lips for fear of disturbing him. There was no resentment in the old man's heart, no regret for the loss of a few trifling valuables, only a compassionate yearning to save a guest from the consequences of his folly.

All night long the warlord dreamed. Picture after picture arose in his mind of happiness enjoyed during previous lives; always there was someone who treated him lovingly – a mother, sister, dear friend and so forth – but each of these tender episodes was followed by one of a heart-rending kind in which he saw someone who had cared for him in the guise of one of his countless victims; time after time he had to endure the pain of reliving his acts of torturing, shooting or beheading someone whom he now recognised as a generous benefactor in one of his former lives. It was unutterably horrible to see himself first as a gay little boy being fondled by an adoring mother, then as the brutal violator or executioner of that dearly loved person in another, but still recognisable, guise; no matter how moving her tears and lamentations, he could not stay his hand.

With the first light of dawn he awoke, body drenched in sweat, mind clouded by self-loathing. Down on his knees he fell before the statue of the Compassionate Kuan Yin and beat his head on the flagstones in a frenzy of remorse. Meanwhile, following instructions given the night before, the boy led his horse from the stable and made ready the saddle-bags bulging with sequestered valuables. Having seen to this, he helped the old lama bring their guest a breakfast of hot tea and such simple fare as that poor place afforded. Then, to the child's great astonishment, the once truculent warrior, bowed to the floor before the lama and pleaded to be accepted as his disciple.

'No', was the reply. 'The monastic life is not for you as yet. Ride on your way. If at any time your fortunes improve, use your power and wealth for the welfare of the oppressed, remembering that every one of them has been your father or your mother or your friend in one of your previous lives, for the lives of all sentient beings stretch back for innumerable eons.'

Startled by the close connection between these words and his recent nightmare, the warlord implored the lama to give him something to hold by in the years to come, whereupon the old man answered:

'There is nothing in the universe stronger than the power of compassion. Hold only to that. Should your efforts sometimes falter owing to your load of evil karma, let the words of Kuan Yin's mantra, OṀ MAṆI PADME HŪṀ, be the seal of your pact never to give rein again to cruelty or avarice.'

So the warlord, after shamefacedly restoring the loot, departed. It is said that, years later, some of his old subordinates came upon him earning his rice as a muleteer employed by a community of monks dwelling in a remote monastery on Wu T'ai's southern peak.

By non-initiates the Mani is often used as a protective charm against all manner of misfortune, whether one's own or another's. It is uttered sharply at moments of danger, gently intoned when comforting someone in afflication and endlessly recited mentally or aloud by those who seek rebirth in the Pure Land. Countless Tibetans die with the Mani upon their lips. There are also many special applications of the mantra. Recently Mr Lu K'uan-yü wrote to me of its remedial use in dealing with repeated hallucinations and similar psychic ills. The sufferer should make it a daily practice to sit facing a bowl of water and, wholeheartedly invoking Avalokiteshvara, gaze at it fixedly for a while, meanwhile reciting the Mani. When a lotus is seen rising from the water, a cure is assured. I myself was enabled to recover in the space of one evening from an illness that beset me during a week-long ride through the mountains in north China. Having tumbled from my mule and been assisted to the nearest inn, I recovered consciousness to discover a Mongolian lama seated by my bed softly intoning OM MANI PADME HUM. Marvellously soothed, I felt fatigue and illness fall away and the following morning set out feeling as fit as on the first day of the journey. It could be argued that the mantra's effect in such circumstances is purely psychological. Indeed that is true, but in a sense that is not altogether simple. The energy of compassion personified by Avalokiteshvara is real and resides at a deep level of one's consciousness; it is present in everyone, however heavily overlaid by ego-born hindrances, and is stirred by the syllables especially when they are pronounced with deep aspiration for another's weal. For some reason, this energy is more easily evoked than similar energies for which there are other mantras; hence the Mani's wide popularity among those who have not received the yogic training on which the effectiveness of those others depends.

The Mani can also be used at higher levels of practice and not a few learned lamas hold it to be the mantra of mantras, entirely sufficient in itself, provided one knows the yogic means of using it effectively. Despite appearances, no magical operation is involved. The mantra, besides having a psychic affinity to an element embedded within the user's consciousness and to an identical element in the psyche of those upon whom it is employed, derives enormous force from the cumulative power of the sacred associations with which it has been invested by the minds of countless people during the course of centuries.

In relating what follows about some of the yogic uses of the Mani, I am anticipating somewhat so as to keep nearly all that is said about this mantra in one place. According to Mahayana doctrine as interpreted by the Vajrayana Sect, the supreme energy welling forth from the Ultimate Source – and hence from the depths of the adept's own consciousness – has two aspects; the wisdom of sacred realisation and the wisdom of compassion. The latter is often personified by Amitabha Buddha of whom Avalokiteshvara is recognised as a divine emanation. Of Avalokiteshvara Bodhisattva's innumerable forms, the one most frequently contemplated is that of a beneficient four-armed deity, pure white in colour, two hands clasping a jewel placed palm to palm in the gesture of prayer, two hands upraised to right and left, of which one clasps a string of crystal beads symbolic of contemplation, the other a lotus signifying spiritual perfection. Successful contemplation does not, however, require careful reflection upon the symbolism; that there are profound yogic reasons for the deity's form, posture, gestures, colours and attributes is taken for granted by those who recognise that the contemplative tradition evolved in Nalanda centuries ago and maintained in Tibet until today contains nothing that is merely fanciful or arbitrary. Except at the start of yogic practice little thought is given to the matter, because dwelling upon interpretation of the symbolism is apt to be distracting; what is needed is to allow the symbols to act directly upon a deeper level of consciousness. The Bodhisattva's lovely Kuan Yin (Kannon) form familiar to all lovers of Chinese and Japanese art is similarly a product of yogic intuition; but artists unaware that Kuan Yin is a meditation deity and not a goddess may have introduced fanciful details not to be found in paintings or statues specially intended as supports to contemplation.

By those with some knowledge of yogic contemplative methods or those who are able to imbue the Compassionate One's form with power arising from the associations it arouses in their minds, the Mani may be used at any time without special preparation. Its recitation by adepts is generally accompanied by visualisation of the deity's form and of the syllables, each with its appropriate colour; simultaneously there arises in the adept's mind a deep yearning for the weal of sentient beings and a longing to experience compassion for them all – compassion not just for those easy to love such as friends, horses, elephants and, puppies, but also for such formerly repellent creatures as noxious insects, reptiles, soldiers, bandits, ghosts and demons. At first, though unable to love them, one can at least sympathise with their sorrows and rejoice in their transient joys, seeing them as fellow-beings doomed like oneself to wander from birth to birth, eon upon eon until Enlightenment is won. Former objects of the yogin's dislike, enmity or peculiar aversion must be given first place as recipients of the Mani's power, the adept directing his mind towards them with all the love of which he is capable. Filled with sorrow for the burdens all must bear and longing for universal happiness, he gazes upon the lovely features of the Bodhisattva, now radiantly visible to his inner eye, and recites over and over again OM MANI PADME HŪM! Or, if he has learnt it from a Tibetan teacher, UM MANI PEME HŪNG!

(The vowel Ū is similar to the first vowel in the English word 'woman'; A is pronounced as in 'father'; PEME, a contraction of PADME, sounds much like 'pay-may', except that the P comes rather close to being a B.)

OM, symbolising the origin, the Supreme Source, the Dharma-kaya, the Absolute, is a powerfully creative word often held to be the sum of all sounds in the universe – the harmony of the spheres, perhaps.

MANI PADME (jewel in the lotus) signify such pairs of concepts as: the essential wisdom lying at the heart of Buddhist doctrine; the esoteric wisdom of the Vajrayana contained within the exoteric Mahayana philosophy; Mind contained within our minds; the eternal in the temporal; the Buddha in our hearts; the goal (supreme wisdom) and the means (compassion); and, if I may be permitted to draw an inference, the Christ Within who dwells in the mind of the Christian mystic.

HŪM is the conditioned in the unconditioned (being to OM as Tê is to Tao in Taoist philosophy); it represents limitless reality embodied within the limits of the individual being, thus it unites every separate being and object with universal OM; it is the deathless in the ephemeral, besides being a word of great power that destroys all ego-born hindrances to understanding.

Such interpretations are naturally of interest, but it is neccessary to stress that reflection upon the symbolism forms no part of the contemplative practice. The mantric syllables cannot produce their full effect upon the deepest levels of the adept's consciousness if his mind is cluttered with verbal concepts. Reflective thought must be transcended, abandoned.

As to the manner of recitation, there can be no fast rules apart from those imposed by one's own teacher, should he choose to do so. The syllable OM is generally emphatic and more or less prolonged so that the final Ṁ vibrates. MAŃI PADME (or MANI PEME) are recited almost as one word. HUM (or HŪNG) is sometimes protracted. One might picture the rhythm thus: _ _ _ _ _ _____! The mantra may be uttered in a monotone; or with OṀ rather higher in pitch than the rest; or with the first five syllables low and monotonous in pitch but with the HŪM pitched as high above the rest as soh is above doh in our musical scale, in which case the diagram would change to _ _ _ _ _‾‾‾‾!

When the recitation comes to an end, the devotee allows the mental picture of the Bodhisattva to fade from his mind in accordance with whatever method he has been taught, then reflects with gratitude on the results, such as enhancement of his power to generate compassion and bestow it impartially, deeper and more sympathetic insight into the hearts of afflicted beings (or of some being or beings in particular), or alleviation of pain, sorrow or mental confusion in the mind of the person to whom the adept's aspiration was directed. Before rising to his feet, he must be sure to perform the mental act of dedicating the merit resulting from his practice to the welfare of all beings, that being the essential conclusion to all yogic practices and rites.

One popular method of employing the Mani is to generate compassion towards all beings in the universe by directing the mind to each of the six states of existence in turn, meanwhile repeating the mantra very slowly perhaps 21 or 108 times; in response to OṀ, white rays shine upon the world of devas; to MA, green rays upon the realm of asuras (titans); to ŃI, yellow rays upon the human realm; to PAD, blue rays upon the realm of animals; to ME, red rays upon the realm of pretas (fiery-mouths); and to HŪM, dark smoky rays upon the denizens of (mind-created) hell. The syllables are visualised as revolving slowly within the Bodhisattva's heart, each shedding its rays in the appropriate direction as it comes to the fore.

The natural inclination of Chinese devotees to contemplate compassion in female form is shared by many Tibetans, who therefore contemplate Tara, an emanation of Avalokiteshvara. According to the individual's need, Tara is variously depicted as a motherly figure of great beauty or as a lovely young maiden.

The method of contemplating her is similar to that used for contemplating other Yidams (forms of the indwelling deity) as described in a later chapter. Here, returning to the *popular* use of mantras, I shall list those pertaining to the twenty-one forms in which Tara is invoked by those seeking protection from one or another calamity. They are:

The Green Tara (source of the other twenty emanations): UM TARE TÜTARE TURE SOHA

The Tara Who Averts Disasters: UM BANZA TARE SARVA BIGANEN SHINDHAM KURU SOHA

The Tara Who Averts Earth-born Calamities: UM TARE TÜTARE TURE MAMA SARVA LAM LAM BHAYA SHINDHAM KURU SOHA

The Tara Who Averts Destruction Wrought by Water: UM TARE TÜTARE TURE MAMA SARVA BHAM BHAM DZALA BHAYA SHINDHAM KURU SOHA

The Tara Who Averts Destruction Wrought by Fire: UM TARE TÜTARE TURE MAMA SARVA RAM RAM DZALA BHAYA SHINDHAM KURU SOHA

The Tara Who Averts Destruction Caused by Wind: UM TARE TÜTARE TURE MAMA SARVA YAM YAM DZALA BHAYA SHINDHAM KURU SOHA

The Tara Who Increases Wisdom: UM RATANA TARE SARVA LOKA JANA PITEYA DARA DARA DIRI DIRI SHÊNG SHÊNG DZA DZANJIA NA BU SHÊNG KURU UM

The Tara Who Averts Heaven-born Calamities: UM TARE TÜTARE TURE MAMA SARVA EH EH MAHA HANA BHAYA SHINDHAM KURU SOHA

The Tara Who Averts Destruction Caused by Armies: UM TARE TÜTARE TURE MAMA SARVA DIK DIK DIKSHENA RAKSHA RAKSHA KURU SOHA

The Tara Who Averts Hell-born Calamities: UM TARE TÜTARE TURE MAMA SARVA RANDZA DUSHEN DRODA SHINDAM KURU SOHA

The Tara Who Averts Evil Caused by Robbers: UM TARE TÜTARE TURE SARVA DZORA BENDA BENDA DRKTUM SOHA

The Tara Who Increases Power: UM BEMA TARE SENDARA HRI SARVA LOKA WASHUM KURU HO

The Tara Who Averts Evil Caused by Demons: UM TARE TÜTARE TURE SARVA DUSHING BIKANEN BHAM PEH SOHA

The Tara Who Averts Evil Affecting Cattle: UM TARE TÜTARE

TURE SARVA HAM HAM DUSHING HANA HANA DRASAYA
PEH SOHA
The Tara Who Averts Evil Caused by Wild Beasts: UM TARE
TÜTARE TURE SARVA HEH HEH DZALEH DZALEH BENDA
PEH SOHA
The Tara Who Averts the Evil Effects of Poison: UM TARE TÜTARE
TURE SARVA DIKSHA DZALA YAHA RAHA RA PEH SOHA
The Tara Who Subdues Demons: UM GARMA TARE SARWA
SHATDRUM BIGANEN MARA SEHNA HA HA HEH HEH HO
HO HUNG HUNG BINDA BINDA PEH
The Tara Who Heals Sickness: UM TARE TÜTARE TURE SARVA
DZARA SARVA DHUKKA BRASHA MANAYA PEH SOHA
The Tara Who Bestows Longevity: UM TARE TÜTARE TURE
BRAJA AYIU SHEI SOHA
The Tara Who Bestows Prosperity: UM TARE TÜTARE TURE
DZAMBEH MOHEH DANA METI SHRI SOHA
The Wish-Fulfilling Tara: UM TARE TÜTARE TURE SARVA
ATA SIDDHI SIDDHI KURU SOHA

These twenty-one mantras have been transcribed in accordance with the Tibetan pronunciation. Final Es must be voiced;
e.g. TARE is pronounced 'ta-rey'. The syllables SOHA
represent the Sanskrit word 'svāhā'; PEH represents the
Sanskrit 'phat'; and, of course, UM represents 'om'. However,
for a reason that will presently become apparent, correct
pronunciation is not of great importance, provided one avoids
elementary mistakes such as pronouncing TARE as though it
had but one syllable like the English word 'tare'.

The effectiveness of these twenty-one mantras has been
attested by too many people for it to be dismissed with a smile,
but it took me some time to arrive at a distinction between them
and the abracadabra of our Western fairy-stories. Later I learnt
that they are held to operate by reason of their affinities with
certain elements of consciousness deeper than the level of conceptual thought. Even so, I am still doubtful as to *how* they
operate. Do they achieve results in a manner analogous to the
shattering of a pane of glass by plucking a lute-string tuned to
the right note (in which case they must surely be imbued with
a power not wholly to be explained by such affinities), or do
they act, not on external circumstances, but on the being of the

mantra-wielder by inspiring a faith that enhances his power to cope with those circumstances? Tibetans adduce persuasive evidence of the former, but the latter is easier to accept. Two ideas being mooted in the modern West are (i) that *all* illness is largely psychosomatic and (ii) that there are psychological means of reducing 'accident proneness'. If one accepts those premises, it is not too far-fetched to suppose that a mantra, by unlocking a hitherto unsuspected force within the psyche, can modify vulnerability to illness or external danger. However, this relatively scientific way of looking at the matter leaves out of account a large number of spectacular effects claimed for mantric yoga, such as the ability to cause or avert hail-storms! Some speculation about this extraordinary aspect of mantras will be found in the final chapter; not that it is of great consequence; such marvels are adjudged by the lamas to be of trivial importance compared to the uses to which mantras are put by those dedicated to man's supreme attainment, winning Enlightenment. As my interest in the true purpose of mantras waxed, so did my eagerness to behold external marvels wane – though I must confess it has never become dormant!

My first meeting with Nyingmapa lamas took place in Sikkim, a land of precipitous green valleys nestling beneath the lovely snow-fields of Kanchenjunga. Unlike Tibet, there are no great monasteries, but hermitages consisting of a small temple surrounded by the wooden cottages of the lamas, who might be monks or married laymen. But for some previous knowledge of the Vajrayana, I might easily have come to share the misconception perpetuated by Western travellers returned from the Himalayan region, namely that here was a form of Buddhism so thickly encrusted with magic and demonology as to be scarcely recognisable as a manifestation of the Sacred Dharma. The rather gloomy interiors of the little temples did contain some likenesses of the Buddhas and Bodhisattvas with the serene expressions familiar to all Buddhists, eyes half-closed, lips touched with smiles betokening inner bliss; but there were many more pictures of demonic beings with cruel horns and fangs, lolling tongues and blazing eyes, innumerable hands grasping a grisly panoply of weapons or displaying such dreadful objects as upturned skulls brimming with fresh blood.

Adorned with necklaces of bones or severed heads, they pranced upon mounds of corpses both animal and human or of writhing bodies freshly disembowelled! What seemed to have escaped the eyes of many writers adumbrating the subject of 'Tibetan religious depravity' were the expressions and bearing of the lamas – these pious men, so far from being wretches lost in horrid fantasies of lust, cruelty and fear, had a most winning manner; kind, generous, easily moved to laughter, they had none of the tight-lipped solemnity nor the determined good-fellow-ship one so often finds among priests in other lands; and their eyes reflected gentleness and wisdom born of long communion with the peace that lies within. Seeing them thus, I put aside any lingering doubts and, accepting in good faith what puzzled or dismayed me, allowed my lamas to lead me where they would. It was well that I did so, for the lamas I encountered in Sikkim and those others under whom I studied later in Kalimpong and elsewhere had a wealth of gifts to offer – treasures of living, treasures of mind. If I have made too little use of the sacred knowledge they took such trouble to impart, the fault has not been theirs.

Had I come to those Nyingmapa lamas ready to accept their teaching only on my own terms or in terms of the rationalism implanted in me in school, had I been unwilling to put some faith in claims unsupported by what I considered scientific evidence, had I insisted in adhering to a strictly logical approach, I suppose I should have learnt nothing. Vajrayana adepts, being dedicated to the perception within their own minds of absolute truth, do employ methods seemingly more akin to magic than to science, holding what is imagined and therefore mind-born to be no less real than the material world – also conceived of as mind-born. At first I had doubts and private reservations, but presently I came to see that, whereas what Mahayanists term relative truth (that is, 'factual truth' about what we call the 'real world') is the province of science and logic, it is the function of a spiritual doctrine to point to absolute truth which, pertaining to the non-dual, indivisible, unmeasurable, can be experienced by intuition but never grasped by conceptual thought – hence the yogin's reliance on vivid imagery, on con-templation of the seemingly 'make-believe'; he must clothe the intangible in forms and colours of which the mind can take hold while it struggles free of the mental grooves worn by applying it only to the tangible. Imagination thus becomes a more precious instrument than thought.

Passing beyond doctrinal teaching, the Vajrayana lays emphasis on direct intuitive experience. Through a specialised form of contemplation, its adepts go deeper than the so-called immutable laws governing the external environment. There are scientists as well as mystics who recognise the purely relative validity of those laws – as Einstein did. Perhaps science itself will one day establish, or at least corroborate, the need for a remarkable depth of mystical perception on the part of those who desire to unveil the face of reality. To most Westerners, mystical perception as a means of arriving at truth is a concept now so unfamiliar that we may be forgiven for finding the training required for its attainment utterly bizarre. Another reason why intelligent Western travellers have been apt to regard the Vajrayana as a hotchpotch of superstition is that it contains so many close parallels to the folk-lore that everywhere preceded scientific knowledge as to seem no more than a survival of ancient ignorance; but, as the pupils of C. G. Jung well know, the imagery of folk-lore is of immense psychological significance; those who discard or refuse to heed it suffer irreparable loss.

Although my lamas were much more concerned with the subjective effects of mantras upon the adept's own mind than with the accomplishment of miraculous feats with the aid of mantric power, they never seemed to doubt the possibility of the latter, however much they might discourage unfruitful curiosity about the subject. In one breath they would confirm that such feats were quite often performed; in another they would chide me for asking to be allowed to witness one. Whether I should ultimately have concluded that their reluctance to give even a tiny demonstration was due to lack of confidence in their own powers, I do not know. Before anything like outright disbelief could crystallise in my mind, I stumbled upon something that struck me as at least partial corroboration of the power of mantras to achieve objective results. By chance I found that mantric control of dreams is possible. It can be argued that what occurs in dreams is altogether subjective since the entire drama is played out in the dreamer's mind; yet there is *a kind of* objectivity involved, since dreams cannot normally be consciously controlled and their content may be strongly at variance with the dreamer's wishes.

To make the matter clear, I must anticipate by touching upon a subject that properly belongs to the next chapter, namely the Yidam or deity who dwells within. Yogas involving the Yidam are based upon a principle which can be stated thus:

Look within! No Buddha, Bodhisattva or deity, no divine force high or low can help your attainment of Enlightenment from without. Mind is the King. Your own mind constitutes your only source of wisdom and yogic power. Therefore, know your mind, recognising in it all that is holy and worthy of highest reverence. For your mind is also Mind, the very substance of the limitless – eternal, non-dual, the Absolute itself! Unfortunately, the self-conquest entailed in coming to know your own mind is the hardest task imaginable. Therefore conjoined with wisdom must be means. All the symbolism of the great Vajrayana system stems from these two – wisdom, the Goal; wisdom and means conjoined, the Path. Truly the teaching of the Buddha leads to Enlightenment, but not until it has been abandoned, leaving wisdom to function from within.

An important yogic application of this principle is to visualise within oneself a deity personifying an aspect of the reality discoverable beneath the layers of ego-born delusion. This meditation deity is conceived of in whatever form one's lama deems well suited to the pupil's needs; it personifies the divine potentiality with which every creature is endowed, the essence of being to be found within each individual while yet transcending all individual bounds, being non-dual, infinite, eternal. The Yidam assigned to me was the Green Tara; the rite for invoking her involved very frequent repetition of her mantra, so that OM TĀRE TŪTĀRE TURE SWĀHĀ would come to revolve constantly in my mind, no matter what thought might be engaging my attention. Though at the time of the episode now to be described I had not reached the point at which the mantra revolves spontaneously, I had come near enough to that for it to spring instantly to mind and lips at moments of crisis.

1   The Twenty-One Taras

2 Shakyamuni Buddha

3 Yamāntaka

4 Avalokiteshvara
(left)
The White Tara
(right)

5 The Precious
Guru (in
youthful
guise) (*left*)
The Precious
Guru (in
characteristic
guise)
(*right*)

6 Manjushri

7 Amitayus Buddha (a meditation form of Amitabha Buddha)

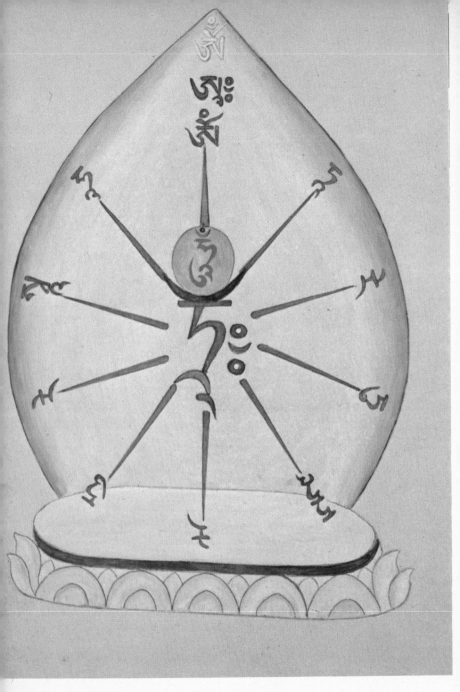

8   Tara's Mantra

Since childhood I have from time to time been visited by nightmares during which I may be menaced by implacable enemies, or cower back as buildings all around me fall in flames beneath a hail of bombs, or see raging jets of fire shoot up as the ground in all directions trembles and gives way. Sometimes I find myself being escorted to a place of execution, a prey to such mournful thoughts as taking last leave of the rising sun, worrying as to how my children will bear the shame of their father's execution or my youngest daughter manage without me. Occasionally I am beset by serpents or seized by vampires. Always these nightmares are full of horridly realistic detail and my emotions are those of a man really caught in one of those grim predicaments. Such dreams still afflict me now and then, but they have lost a good deal of their power to terrify; for one night I made the discovery that a sharp ejaculation of Tara's mantra instantly cuts off whatever danger may be threatening. I seldom wake at that point, but the threatening circumstance is dealt with and the dream takes a pleasant course, during which I behold a mountainous island rising from a foam-capped sea – Tara's Potala in the Southern Ocean – or some similarly delightful scene of which the colours especially are infinitely lovelier than anything known to me in waking life.

Occasionally the pattern differs. Not long ago I dreamt that I had been brought to a place of confinement from which the sole egress lay through a well-guarded door. Somehow I knew that I had been unjustly consigned to a home for the mentally afflicted – a scaffold would have seemed less mournful! The attendants obviously took a sadistic pleasure in my frantic appeals to be released. As usual, the Yidam's mantra did not arise in my mind until I had reached the point of absolute despair. The recollection brought a moment of great joy; but, this time, before I had time to utter it, one of my sneering captors pronounced it himself, adding with a grin: 'What are you waiting for? By all means call upon your precious Yidam, if you care to waste your breath.' I was appalled! Never had I felt such cruel despondency. Almost I abandoned my Yidam, but not quite. Scarcely daring to hope, I uttered the mantra. Though the immediate effect was merely to excite a derision which vanquished whatever slender thread of hope remained, within seconds I was walking through the window unimpeded by its bars!

Some years before being visited by that dream, I had made another discovery that convinced me of the psychic effectiveness of my Yidam's mantra. A friend interested in the apparent similarity between yogic experience and the states induced by hallucinogens persuaded me to try mescalin. The drug's effect on me was terrifying – so much so that I wonder if anyone has ever experienced a worse 'trip' than mine! Fully aware of my surroundings and, during the early stages, still able to talk, eat and drink, I underwent a shattering disintegration accompanied by mental torment that was well-nigh unendurable. I would have given anything in the world for a means of immediate relief, but it was a public holiday and we might have driven all over the city of Bangkok without finding a doctor who would treat a wound made by a rabid dog, let alone waste a moment on delivering a fool from the consequences of his own folly – or so I believed, though that in itself was probably a hallucination. For hours the agony continued, intensifying rather than abating. Quite literally I longed to die! At last, in a spirit of total self-abandonment, I called piteously upon my Yidam, using of course her mantra. In a flash, the situation was transformed! Horror gave place to bliss of the same high order of intensity!

I shall relate one more experience of a different kind, except that my Yidam's mantra again played its part. In itself the incident would be too trivial to be worth relating, were it not that, for the first time, the mantra produced an effect that was wholly external to myself. Boasting of yogic power is not only impious but a sure way of losing it; however, in this case, no boasting is involved, for the result, being unintentional, reflects no special skill on my part, but only the power of the mantra itself.

I had come to spend a few days with a friend who had in his apartment in Hong Kong an ancient and lovely statue of the Green Tara. Before going to bed, I asked for incense and a bowl of water for use in a brief rite which one of my lamas had ordered me to perform every day of my life without fail. My friend, whom I had known since meeting him at the Forest of Recluses when both of us were very young, was a deeply

erudite Buddhist scholar, but not well acquainted with the Vajrayana. Out of curiosity, he asked if he might be present while
I performed the rite, and to this I most willingly assented; so
we sat together side by side on cushions placed before the shrine
wherein he had placed his Green Tara image. As usual, I lighted
incense sticks and then proceeded with what was intended to
be a purely mental transformation of the bowl of water into an
ocean of the liquid that symbolises wisdom. To my knowledge,
nothing unexpected occurred; but, when we had risen from our
final prostrations, my friend – without much surprise – quietly
remarked that, during my mantric recitation, the water in the
bowl had turned green – Tara's colour! The mantra had never
had that effect before, nor was it intended to achieve any kind
of physical transformation of the water. Undoubtedly the
phenomenon resulted from the conjunction of the mantra's
power and that residing in the antique statue. As my thoughts
had been turned inwards and I had not been looking at the water
in the bowl, I cannot say whether it actually turned green, or
did so only in the mind of my friend; in either case, the effect
was external in that the mantra I uttered caused something to
happen outside myself. The incident had a certain influence
on my ability to credit stories of much more spectacular mantric
happenings; trifling though it was, it was *of the same order* as
those spectacular events in which I had found it so difficult to
believe.

Chapter 4

The Indwelling Deity

My recollections of scenes that marked stages in the gradual unfolding of my knowledge of yoga are not always of gatherings in temples, either great or small. As was to be expected, some precious insights dawned during the hours I spent in my shrine-room here in Bangkok. I particularly remember my joy when, a few months after I had begun to practice contemplative yoga, for the first time everything happened as it should, probably because I had learnt to do what must be done *effortlessly.* I was sitting before my private altar, whereon candles flickered in a pair of silver Tibetan butter-lamps and incense smouldered in an oblong censer with a perforated design in the form of the mantra OM MAṄI PADME HŪM so that the smoke would rise in the shape of each of those syllables in turn as the sticks gradually burnt away. *Tormas* there were none, for I have never learnt how to make them, but token offerings of such substances as pure water, grain, flowers and fruit were ranged in little silver bowls. Though none of these objects was essential to the yoga, it was pleasant to have them; shrine-rooms should be made to look as clean and attractive as possible. Behind the altar hung a *thanka* depicting the Green Tara, my chosen Yidam, embodiment of 'the Buddha in my heart'. Softly I recited her mantra, seeing in my mind the figure of the living Tara with the bija-mantra TĀM blazing at the centre of her heart. Round it revolved the syllables OM TĀRE TŪTĀRE TURE SWĀHĀ, a shining band of cool green fire, their motion distilling a white nectar which, passing through the crown of my head, penetrated downwards driving out impurities in the form of black smoke and transforming my body into a crystal vase brimming with elixir whiter than snow. Presently the glowing syllables withdrew into the TĀṂ, the TĀṂ dissolved and naught was left but to enter objectless awareness.

Contemplation of the indwelling deity, embodiment of our innate divinity, forms the very foundation of mantric yoga

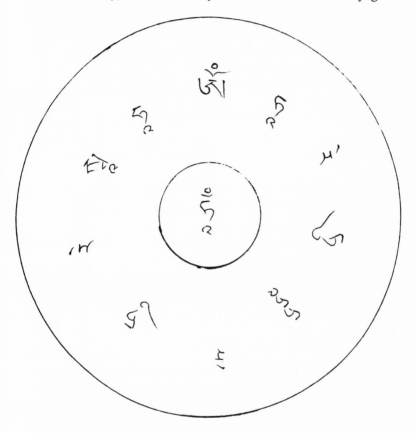

aimed at the swift attainment of Enlightenment. The manner of evoking this deity was long kept secret and is still taught with circumspection. Even now, initiation can hardly be dispensed with; besides ensuring correct instruction, it confers *empowerment* – a transmission of the yogic virtue of one's lama and of his whole line of predecessors stretching back, in the case of Nyingmapas and Kargyupas, to the Precious Guru, Padma Sambhava, and even to Shakyamuni Buddha himself. In Europe and America, initiation is no longer very hard to obtain, now that some of the refugee lamas have settled there.

Initiations also serve another purpose, namely ensuring that no harm results from improper conduct of the yogic rites. Like other powerful forces, mantric yogas can be used either to build or to destroy. Their destructive function is properly aimed at inner hindrances to Enlightenment, the karmic load of this and former lives, but mantras can be inadvertently misused with dangerous consequences and there have been yogins who have deliberately abused their knowledge to accomplish perverted ends. Therefore all the Buddhist esoteric sects – the Indo-Tibetan Vajrayana, the Japanese Shingon and, while it lasted, the Chinese Mi Tsung – have confined mantric instruction to initiates. To this day, the methods of employing many important mantras are guarded from the uninitiated; and though others, such as OM MANI PADME HŪM, are very widely used, they are *formally* communicated only after two steps have been taken – first a minor *wang* (empowerment), second a *loong* or oral transmission of words which must be spoken by the lama into the disciple's ear. During most *wangs*, a pledge of secrecy is given. That the requirements for initiation have been considerably relaxed and that permission to write about yogic subjects is no longer difficult to obtain are both largely due to the Chinese occupation of Tibet, for the death or exile of so many lamas has aroused concern about the future transmission of the sacred knowledge. Another reason is that the lamas, moved by a spirit of compassion, are especially accommodating to the needs of foreign pupils, who can seldom stay close to a lama long enough to win his trust and approval in the old manner.

Fortunately deliberate abuse of mantras by Western adepts is unlikely. In the first place, it is not easy to acquire the techniques needed for producing dire results; in the second, those who have no reverence for mantras will scarcely bother with them, while those who have are generally aware of the dangers of abuse. Mantric yoga is part of a tradition which recognises that all activities of body, speech and mind, both good and bad, produce consequences which the doer cannot possibly escape. Improper use of yogic knowledge brings retribution in its train. The karmic load of an adept who employs mantras to bring about an enemy's destruction is doubly heavy – to the evil of seeking to take life is added that of profaning sacred knowledge. The biography of Milarepa relates how painfully his teacher, Marpa, punished the poet's profanation of mantric knowledge when as a youth he had used it to destroy the persecutors of his family. Before vouchsafing him even a crumb of teaching, Marpa made the young man suffer years of harsh servitude, requiring him to build house after house upon distant hill-tops with mud and stones taken from afar and then immediately commanding him to pull them down and carry back the mud and stones to their original places. Muscles aching, limbs and shoulders covered with abrasions, the unhappy youth complied. Marpa, of course, was exercising compassion; causing Milarepa bitter suffering in his present life was the most effective way of reducing the karmic load resulting from his shocking abuse of powers gained through yoga.

I could not describe the baneful use of mantras even if I perversely desired to do so, for my gentle teachers never dreamed of transmitting such knowledge. What is much more to be feared is unintentional misuse, an important reason for acquiring the careful instruction that follows upon initiation.

That which distinguishes the mystic's way from more widely trodden religious paths is recognition that Enlightenment – Liberation, Salvation – comes from within himself. Herein lies the key to the highest knowledge. It is with this in mind that one must seek true understanding of mantras and all other aids to yogic progress. Broadly speaking, there are two separate concepts of this truth. Whereas Christian and Moslem mystics, understanding mystical experience in the light of their own dogmas, conceive of *attaining* union with God, Buddhists and Taoists conceive of *realising* Nirvana or the Tao. The different ways of naming the goal are of no great importance, but there is a wide notional difference between attainment and realisation: the former suggests a separation between the devotee and his goal which has to be bridged; the latter implies a union that has never ceased to be, even though, shrouded by ego-born delusions, it remains unperceived until realisation takes place. Even so, the actual experience, whether termed attainment or realisation, does not differ, for it is a product of the direct intuition of Ultimate Truth.

Buddhists and Taoists enjoy the advantage that there is no conflict between those who adhere to mystical and non-mystical approaches. In theory at least, all Buddhism is mystical; for, not recognising an omnipotent creator, it teaches that there is no one to please, offend, placate and that consequently all attainment must take place within the devotee's own being. The Mahayana School of Buddhism, of which the Vajrayana forms a part, goes further by proclaiming that the entire universe results from the play of Mind. Mind is the only reality and the seeming individuality of our finite minds results from ignorance of our true nature arising from primordial delusion. This conception of the universe is shared by certain Hindu sects, which employ a somewhat different kind of mantric yoga; but, having not been initiated into any of them, I cannot describe their yoga from direct knowledge, so I have thought it best not to attempt a description.

Accomplished mystics, despite differences in the terminology they employ, recognise that the experience of mystical union is the same for all; in becoming accomplished, they have risen above conflicting dogmas, prejudice and controversy. On the other hand, those who have yet to taste the mystic's joy may be puzzled as to what motivates a uniquely inward approach to wisdom. Many question the need for any kind of spiritual activity other than observance of a reasonable code of morality. Some would discard even that much.

In the case of a fortunate few, mystical experience arises of itself, conferring such bliss that these questions appear ludicrous. Next in good fortune are those in whom not the experience but a great thirst for it spontaneously arises; though tormented while it remains unquenched, they are comforted by an intuitive foreknowledge of the bliss that can be won. But what of the rest – that is to say, most people? Not much reflection is required to realise the unsatisfactoriness of life, how much of it is boring, if not downright painful or tragic, how fleeting are its satisfactions, how often disappointed are its shining hopes. Faced with this drab, often grim, reality, generations of our ancestors sought refuge in piety and in the belief that heaven would provide compensation for their earthly woes. Today, however, such simple beliefs have lost their power to comfort. But what if there is a religion beyond religions, a shining, living truth, the true inspiration of all religions though so often mis-apprehended that the light is now rarely seen at all? There is no way to prove to the blind that light exists. They must con-quer their blindness and perceive it for themselves, for it can never be conveyed in words. To me, the first intimation of its existence came when I was caught up in the atmosphere of joyousness and kindness that pervades the persons of those who have spent their lives contemplating what lies within, instead of dissipating their forces on the ceaseless play of phenomena without.

Because so many Tibetans are steeped in an ancient and en-lightened tradition, among the lamas can be found a sufficient number imbued with joy, compassion and inner stillness to convince one that they share a secret infinitely worth knowing. Naturally, neither they nor Buddhists generally have a mono-poly of this secret; I have met Taoists whose faces conveyed that same blissful tranquillity, and I have read accounts of Hindu, Sufi and Christian mystics of similar attainment. It is because Taoists have almost vanished from the earth and accomplished mystics generally are much rarer than before that it makes good sense to seek teachers in the Himalayan border regions where the old contemplative traditions still flourish.

While it is true that the means to mystical accomplishment are not the exclusive property of any faith, Buddhism does offer two special advantages: it refrains from insistence upon set beliefs, which often prove obstacles to spiritual progress; and it provides a whole panoply of contemplative methods for culti-vating intuition of the reality. My personal preference for the Mahayana form of Buddhism is rooted in two circumstances: it offers a wide variety of means suited to different tempera-ments and levels of understanding; even more important, it clearly propounds the doctrine of Mind as Supreme Reality. Within the Mahayana fold, I have found the contemplative yogas of the Vajrayana Sect particularly inspiring; had it been otherwise, I could scarcely have written about mantras, for it is to that sect that one must turn for profound mantric knowledge.

Vajrayana doctrine offers two precious insights into truth, one of them common to all Mahayana sects, the other a once closely guarded secret. They are: recognition of the identity of *samsara* and Nirvana; and a highly esoteric concept – 'I am the Buddha!'

Samsara is the universal flux wherein beings are doomed to wander for as long as the ego-born delusion of independent existence persists, our world being but an infinitesimal fraction of the whole. Nirvana is the ultimate being-non-being beyond human conception and not to be attained until the last shred of ego-delusion has been discarded. Yet *samsara* and Nirvana are not two! There is no going from the one to the other, nor are there any individual beings to make the journey; there is only a falling away of illusion, a sudden recognition of things as they really are, a revelation of the true nature of the self and of all selves that ever could be. To employ a simple analogy – a child born and reared in a pitch-dark room must conceive of his surroundings as devoid of colour and visual form; then light appears and everything seems gloriously different; yet the room is the same, nothing has changed but the child's conception of his surroundings.

'I am the Buddha!' If 'the Buddha' is taken to signify the Ultimate, that which theistic mystics call the Godhead, it will be seen that these tremendous words embody the very essence of mystical perception. One who understands them perceives himself to be both worshipper and worshipped, the individual and the universal, a being seemingly insignificant but in truth divine! From this perception stem three obligations: to treat all beings, however outwardly repugnant, as embodiments of the sacred essence; to recognise all sounds, no matter how they offend the ear, as components of sacred sound; and to recollect that nowhere throughout the universe is other than Nirvana, however dense the dark clouds of illusion. Therefore, whatever befalls, the adept is clothed in divinity; with his eye of wisdom, he perceives the holiness of all beings, all sounds, all objects; and his heart of wisdom generates measureless compassion.

From the moment an aspirant begins seeking deliverance from within, abandons the dualism of worshipper and worshipped and recognises the identity of 'self-power' and 'other-power' as sources of spiritual inspiration, the shackles of ego-consciousness are loosened; and as the power of the illusory ego wanes, the qualities of patience, forebearance and compassion blossom. Even so, great danger inheres in the liberating concept 'I am the Buddha'; improperly understood, it leads to grossly irresponsible behaviour and to overweaning pride which, by inflating the ego instead of diminishing it, enmeshes the aspirant ever more tightly in delusion's bonds. Therefore this knowledge was formerly hidden from the profane and therefore the lamas teach skilful means for counteracting that grave hazard. Never must one reflect 'I am the Buddha' without recalling that, at the level of absolute truth, there is no such entity as 'I'!

Mere acceptance of the doctrine that divinity lies within is a far cry from intuitively experiencing its truth; yet, until that experience dawns, nothing of lasting value has been gained. To accomplish a journey on foot, say from Paris to Lhasa, one starts by taking a step in a southeasterly direction; good, the journey has begun, but one is still as far from Lhasa as citizens who have stepped out from their doors to buy a loaf of bread; one is better off than before the journey was contemplated only in having a plan to go somewhere. So it is with the aspirant. It is because the journey from acceptance to perception of the truth is so fraught with pitfalls that the Vajrayana provides a variety of means for attaining the goal as swiftly as lies within each individual's power. Both the task and the means are psychological, for the long road starts and finishes within the compass of a human skull.

Mantras form part of the skilful means employed from the start of the journey and are used right up to that high point at which 'means' of every kind are discarded. Mantric yoga involves, first and foremost, the adoption of a Yidam, a form wherewith to embody the indwelling deity. To Buddhists of some other sects, be they Zen followers or Theravadins, this may seem a preposterous perversion of one of their most cherished beliefs; for, traditionally, Buddhists have been taught to eschew deities. True, at the popular level, believers often address petitions to the deities of other faiths (Hindu, Taoist and so forth according to locality), but the benefits they seek have nothing to do with spiritual progress. (I once helped a young Presbyterian girl, unhappily in love, to slip into Walsingham Abbey and light candles to the Virgin; the point being that her own faith – like Buddhism – offered no facilities for securing a happy end to a love affair.) According to Buddhist doctrine, since the entire universe results from the play of mind, there can be no omnipotent creator standing apart from it; gods are but one of several orders of being which, though possessed perhaps of enviable powers, are subject to the laws of birth, growth, decay and death in accordance with a time-scale appropriate to their nature. The Buddha often spoke of gods in a context embracing as many worlds as there are grains of sand in the Ganges river; he taught that it was useless to look to them for aid in making spiritual progress, which is wholly dependent on one's own efforts. In other words, one should regard gods somewhat in the light of, say, panthers and dolphins – real enough but belonging to a species of but slight concern to spiritual man.

Not to be confused with gods are the Buddhas and Bodhisattvas of the Mahayana pantheon. These include the historical Buddha; but, for the most part, they are personifications of forces emanating from the wisdom–compassion energy generated by Mind. Thus, wisdom is personified by Manjushri, compassion by Avalokiteshvara, perfect activity by Vajrapani, etc. At the popular level, they are often mistaken for deities and it is convenient to refer to them collectively by that name; but by yogic adepts they are recognised as being simultaneously emanations of all-embracing Mind and, in a sense, creations of one's own mind.

To return to the methods of mantric yoga, though they involve what may look to the outsider very much like theistic rites, they are in fact superb psychological means of achieving direct intuitive realisation of the divinity within our minds. To emphasise the special nature of the objects of contemplation, I often refer to them as 'meditation deities'. Any one of these may be employed as the Yidam or 'indwelling deity' of the individual adept. There are hundreds if not thousands of them and they are arranged in a hierarchy that corresponds to the increasing differentiation of wisdom–compassion energy at progressive distances from the Source. It is vital that the adept learn to recognise that these streams flow from within himself, his seemingly individual mind being no other than infinite Mind; nevertheless he must first visualise them as flowing from outside, Mind being provisionally conceived of as lying somewhere 'beyond'; next, from inside; and finally from both inside and outside, which he now recognises as identical. Mind and his own mind are not two!

To assist him in this realisation (which must go far beyond mere intellectual acceptance), he is allotted a Yidam personifying a differentiated form of wisdom–compassion energy. In Asia especially, unsophisticated aspirants are apt to believe at the outset that their Yidams are self-existing deities who must be invited to take up their abode within; moreover, even sophisticated aspirants are taught to begin by visualising the Yidams *as though* external to themselves; and, at a later stage, they have to alternate that practice with visualisation of the Yidams as internal forces. As adepts rise to higher levels, they must not discard their earlier practices altogether; for, whereas contemplation of an external deity leads to the error of theism, uninterrupted contemplation of the internal deity at a time when understanding is not fully ripened may lead to dire results, giving rise to pride and thus enhancing the ego's power. Also, in a certain restricted sense, the Yidam *is* a separate being – not truly separate from the adept's own mind since Ultimate Source and adept are one, but separate in that the Yidam in some respects belongs to the realm of appearances wherein individual entities do have a transitory existence, for the deity represents not the Source itself but one of the differentiated energies flowing therefrom, energies which bifurcate and redivide as distance from the Source increases. That forces and objects may be at once separate and not separate is well explained by the doctrine of interpenetration contained in the Avatamsaka (Hua Yen) Sūtra, which sets forth how every object in the universe is penetrated by and penetrates every other object. To say that Yidam and adept are separate is wrong in one sense; to say they are identical is wrong in another; hence the need to alternate the two approaches. This is analogous to another profound mystical truth – just as the universe contains each being, so does each being contain the universe. Contemplation of the Yidam as oneself yields perception that is fully valid, but error will be avoided if one adds the perception that arises from contemplating the Yidam as external.

The Yidam allotted to an aspirant whose yogic skills are (like my own) very modest is usually an embodiment of one of the subsidiary streams of wisdom–compassion energy, such as Tara or a *dakini*, for these subsidiary streams are closer to the level of relative truth to which 'every-day' consciousness pertains, so they are easier to grasp than more rarefied energies at only one or two removes from the Source. The emphasis is on practice, not belief. Where direct intuition is the goal, beliefs are of small consquence, so the extent to which an aspirant is aware of the true nature of meditation deities makes little difference to his progress; later, understanding will dawn of itself. This being so, I rather think that yogic contemplation involving evocation of the Yidam could be used effectively by the adherents of any religion; just as the forms of the Yidams visualised by Tibetans are largely borrowed from Indian and Bön iconography, so could those used by Christians or others be borrowed from iconography familiar to them. For such an innovation to become acceptable to the church authorities, the Yidams would have to be represented as psychological aids to intuition; at first, this rather limited conception of the Yidams' nature would not greatly matter; and when intuition arose any errors of understanding would right themselves. Christians could never reconcile themselves to spiritual practices involving the ritual worship of 'heathen deities', but that should prove no obstacle. Since meditation deities are neither more nor less than personifications of intangible energies, they can take any form associated in the adept's mind with holy awe. This, however, is pure speculation; I have never thought to consult either lamas or Christian priests about the matter. Yet the suggestion is not a frivolous one; it would be absurd to suppose that those great mystics of the past who spoke of inspiration by the Holy Spirit, of the Christ Within and of union with the Godhead were talking of something fundamentally different from the path and goal of Buddhist mysticism.

It is in the evocation of meditation deities – often, but not always one's Yidam – that mantras play their greatest role; all others, however spectacular, are purely secondary. Each of these deities has a bija-mantra of one syllable, a heart-mantra composed of several syllables, and sometimes a longer mantra as well, all of which embody the energy which that particular deity personifies.

Bija-mantras, besides being, as it were, the seeds that give birth to the 'transformation scenes' in the mind of the adept that form the substance of yogic visualisations, are also associated with what are known in yoga as the body's psychic centres (*chakra*), and can be employed to stimulate those centres with the energies imbuing them. It is taught that bija-mantras, in particular, owe much of their efficacy to *shabda* (sacred sound), a mysterious force touched upon in the final chapter; moreover, the Lama Govinda informs us that their sounds have a directive quality – upwards or downwards; horizontal or vertical, etc., but this is one of several aspects of mantras which I cannot elucidate for lack of first-hand knowledge.

In yogic contemplation, the chief function of bija-mantras is to direct the energy personified by the Yidam into the initially lifeless image which the adept creates within his own mind. While the heart-mantra is being recited, it is visualised as a circle of brilliantly coloured syllables revolving round the bija-mantra glowing in the Yidam's heart. This visualisation leads – sometimes in a flash – to an experience of union with the deity evoked; but not unless long practice of the yoga has, as it were, filled the glowing mantras with the adept's very life-blood, for there must be a meeting and a blending of the Yidam's energy with the adept's own. The heart-mantras are not arbitrarily invented groups of syllables, but intimately connected both with the energy invoked and with their counterparts in the depth consciousness of the adept; hence their extraordinary power to release the dormant energy of his psyche. When, at a later stage, the deity's true nature is revealed, the veils of illusion are rent and increasingly exalted perceptions follow.

A lama, in choosing a Yidam for each pupil at the time of

his initiation, carefully weighs his special needs. Some Yidams are endowed with superhuman beauty; thus, Tara often appears as an exquisite maiden and both Padma Sambhava (the Precious Guru of the Nyingmapas and Kargyupas) and Man-jushri Bodhisattva (embodiment of wisdom) sometimes appear as lovely youths; indeed, the Precious Guru may even appear as a chubby, rosy-cheeked child not long past infancy. On the other hand, there are Yidams of blood-curdling ferocious aspect, often with many heads and limbs and with all kinds of grisly attributes and ornaments. These portray nothing re-motely resembling the 'wrath of God', but rather the indomit-able powers needed to crush the ingrained passions and evil tendencies wherewith the ego defends itself against valiant efforts to achieve its dissolution. It is taught that at death, when one enters the *bardo* or intermediate state between death and rebirth, one will encounter just such terrifying thought-forms which the yogin, familiar with them during his meditations, will recognise as friends and allies, whereas the foolish will flee from them and thus hasten to enmesh themselves in unsuitable rebirths. In keeping with the all-embracing nature of the Abso-lute from whence these forms descend, even lovely Tara has her grim demonic form and, conversely, the hideous, bull-headed, flaming Yamāntaka may appear as the gentle youth Manjushri; for it is thus that dualism is transcended. Were the adept to cling to beauty and flee from horror, dwell always upon joy and exclude terror from his mind, how would it be possible for him to attain to the non-dual realm? It takes not 'one' but 'both' to lead to 'neither'.

Evocation of the Yidam requires more than the exercise of a trained imagination and recollection of the many significant details. For the pictured form to be imbued with life and confer its power, a mysterious energy must be unlocked by recitation and visualisation of the appropriate mantras. As a result of long practice, accomplished adepts can evoke such deities and mantras instantaneously and draw upon their power even when contemplative yoga is not being performed; but neither recitation nor visualisation is effective unless the deity invoked can be made to 'live'. Merely projecting pictures on the mind is worthless. Yet, perhaps on account of the mantras, the task is easier than some of the other forms of meditative contemplation.

Experienced meditators know how often it happens that a meditation period passes in vain with the mind behaving more like a forest deer than a well-trained steed; thoughts refuse to be dismissed and strenuous effort is required to accomplish what should be effortless. If one who practises Zen or Theravadin meditation often falls into this unsatisfactory state, his resolution may fall away and boredom and inertia follow. In some such cases, the Vajrayana methods sometimes prove a marvellous means of circumventing failure. As one sits reciting the Yidam's mantra and contemplating the glowing syllables revolving and then merging one into another, there may occur a sudden transformation, as when a switch is pressed and light comes flooding into a darkened room; whereupon one is transported into a realm of consciousness beautiful in its serenity, a state of keen awareness which, being devoid of object, is of inconceivable purity.

Ch'an (Zen) and Vajrayana methods, seemingly so different, really have much in common. Both are known as short-path methods on account of their common aim – Enlightenment in this very life. Though their starting points are different, once the realm of conceptual thought is left behind, the paths converge. What is the Yidam but an embodiment of Original Mind, a form used to clothe the inconceivable until the point at which forms are transcended? While Ch'an (Zen) with its austere simplicity is ideally suited to certain temperaments, there are aspirants who find that the colour, sound and movement inherent in Vajrayana contemplative yoga enhance their powers of concentration; naturally such manifestations of differentiated form have ultimately to be transcended, but they themselves mysteriously provide the power to achieve that very purpose – thus the ego's cherished allies are employed for its destruction! The wisdom of Ch'an lies in withdrawal from the field of embattled opposites; the wisdom of the Vajrayana lies in employing the weapons of the antagonists to put to flight their armies; each in its own way leads directly to the non-dual state.

The essence of the preliminary yogic method for achieving

mystical realisation of our true nature by evocation of the in-dwelling deity is thus:

That the yoga may be fully effective, the Yidam is conceived of at the outset as an external deity, for the deluded instinct which makes men search for a god outside themselves must not be violated but satisfied until the aspirant has been led to discard it. Soon he attains direct intuition that the Yidam dwells within; next he perceives his own identity with the Yidam and, at a later stage, recognises the Yidam as being also identical with the Ultimate Source. Thus the separateness of the realms of form and void is discovered, by the use of skilful means, to be illusory. The inconceivable is conceived by embodying it conceptually up to the moment when the need for concepts ceases. This process so closely resembles a child's make-believe that one may wonder why men of superior intellect bother with it instead of starting at the highest level of understanding of which they are capable. The point is that mere *understanding* is worthless; the experience has to unfold at a level deeper than that of the intellect; the techniques for hastening that unfolding are pro-founder than at first appears. Mere ratiocination will not lead to perceptual experience of the truth that, just as the great contains the small, so does the small contain the great, in the sense that the entire compass of this and all possible universes lies within each human skull!

Resorting to make-believe is less rare as a spiritual technique than is generally realised. For example, within the fold of the theistic religions, though God is held to be formless, his wor-shippers generally endow him with some fanciful form; how otherwise could they envisage him at all? The Vajrayana method merely systematises an approach that others use in-stinctively. The Ultimate Source, immeasurable, intangible, devoid of attributes, is naturally beyond conception; therefore subtle means must be employed to grasp it. At first one seeks to comprehend one of its intermediate emanations with charac-teristics pertaining somewhat to the void and somewhat to the realm of form. Herein lies the secret of the Yidam – a form tem-porarily given to the formless and one with attributes upon which the mind can dwell, but not so solid that the voidness of its nature is lost sight of, unless by neophytes who have much to learn. Where the Vajrayana outdistances the theistic religions is in aiming at a degree of perception whereat, not only the form of the deity, but the deity himself comes to be recognised as a wholly provisional concept.

Before rising at dawn, the adept recites the mantra embodying the energy of his Yidam, who is thereby evoked. After his morning ablutions, he repairs to his shrine-room, where such offerings as pure water, flowers, incense, lamps and so forth are ranged before a statue of the Buddha. If possible, there should be a picture or statue of the Yidam. The offerings may be of extreme simplicity (a single flower or bowl of water) or as elaborate as one cares to make them. Having touched his head to the ground three times, the adept mentally converts them into offerings of great magnificence, pronouncing the mantra OM ĀH HŪM as he touches each of them; with these syllables he imbues them with his body, speech and mind, so that each flower or bundle of incense-sticks betokens his total *self-surrender*.

Then follows the taking of the Four Refuges – refuge in the Guru, the Buddha, the Dharma (Doctrine) and the Saṃgha (Sacred Community). Next the adept, reflecting on his imperfections, resolves to abjure them; whereafter he rejoices in the merits of those who have won to supreme attainment. His lama will probably have taught him to perform several other yogic preliminaries of this kind. Then, fixing his mind upon the ultimate goal of his practice, he recites the mantra OM SVA-BHĀVAŚUDDHĀH SARVA DHARMĀH SVABHĀVA ŚUDDHO 'HAM ĀH HŪM, meaning 'Devoid of own-being are all components of existence; devoid of own-being am I'. These syllables, being imbued with mantric power, will assist him to arrive intuitively at the sublime truth they enshrine.

The yogic contemplation of the Yidam comprises mantras, mudras and visualisation and thus engages all three faculties, body, speech and mind. The adept beholds a spotless void wherein suddenly appears a mantric syllable glowing with light. This suddenly becomes a lotus enthroning within its centre the Yidam's bija-mantra. In a flash, this changes to a likeness of the Yidam, every detail of whose form, being clearly visualised, conveys its psychic meaning to the adept's mind. Next, by uttering a mantra, the living Yidam is evoked and, entering the mentally created likeness resting upon the lotus, there dwells. Within the Yidam's heart once more appears the bija-mantra, now encircled by the Yidam's heart-mantra – a revolving band of glowing syllables. Uttering it countless times, the adept contemplates the syllables which, as they revolve, emit rays that shine upon beings in the ten directions; a stream of light enters his body through the crown of his head. Presently the Yidam's form diminishes, passes into the adept also through the crown, and comes to rest in his heart; whereat the adept feels himself diminishing in size until he and the Yidam are coextensive, merged, inseparable, not two. The mantra now revolves within their single heart. Presently the syllables withdraw into the initial OM and this is absorbed by the bija-mantra in the centre, which itself contracts and melts into the minute circle that crowns it. Finally this circle vanishes and naught remains but void, the Yidam-adept having entered *samadhi* – a blissful state of objectless awareness, there to dwell for as long as that state can be effortlessly maintained.

On withdrawing from *samadhi*, the adept offers up various aspirations, which always include a heart-felt longing for the Buddhas and all Enlightened Beings to remain in the universe 'turning the Wheel of the Law'. Lastly, he offers up his own merits for the benefit of all sentient beings.

The Yidam, having united with the adept during the morning yoga, there remains and is retained, if possible, throughout the day. Now that his body has become the temple of that sacred being, the adept reinforces his perception of the unity of worshipper and worshipped by mentally converting all that pleases him – the savour of good food, the coolness of the breeze upon his skin – into offerings to the Yidam. The Yidam's mantra is forever on his lips and in his mind so that, as time goes by, the syllables arise spontaneously. In the evening and perhaps more often, the yoga is repeated and, on retiring to bed, the adept uses the mantra to raise the deity above his head to guard his sleep. He may also mantrically create a *vajra*-tent, a protective pavilion of which the mesh is formed of interlocked *vajra*-sceptres or of the syllables of the Yidam's mantra.

Among the immediate by-products of this yogic practice is

one that is especially esteemed; at moments of crisis, the mantra springs to mind spontaneously with the result that the adept may hope to die with his thoughts fixed upon his Yidam and with the Yidam's mantra upon his lips. Should death occur before he has attained direct intuitive perception of the goal, at the very least he may expect rebirth amidst circumstances that will favour his making further progress.

Should an aspirant desire instruction in the marvellous tantric techniques for transmuting the energies engendered by the passions into potent weapons for their destruction so as to nullify the ego very rapidly, his Yidam is likely to be one of the fierce divinities. It would be especially dangerous to adopt one of them, unless one's lama were always at hand to give guidance, for they embody very powerful energies suited to a difficult and dangerous task, which may easily get out of hand.

Of the higher stages of the yogic path, I cannot say much; my knowledge is very limited and, in any case, it would not be fitting to describe them; but it is possible to hint at the marvellous subjective experiences evoked by mantras in the mind of an accomplished yogin.

There is a bija-mantra which instantly transforms the yogin into the likeness of one of the fierce divinities; he beholds himself as that deity; his being seems to pulse with stupendous power and to have taken on such vastness that worlds are but heaps of shining pebbles in his path. As he utters this mantra, myriads of beings, replicas of his own dread form, pour forth from his body and fill the sky, striking, driving off, obliterating hindrances to yogic progress. Each of those beings is imbued with the energy embodied in that syllable and so great is their number that they fill the universe – not a chink of empty space remains, all objects or semblances which space contains having dissolved with 'a singing and a ringing'. Naught remains of the yogin's flesh but 'a throbbing and a ringing'. Thus are all component entities, within him and without, purged of their illusory separate being.

There are mantras for evoking from the Void syllables that blaze with light-rays like rising suns or send forth brilliant bands of coloured light, which divide and subdivide until 60,000,000 separate beams are projected. From certain syllables issue forth assemblages of deities who fill the sky before being reabsorbed and merged therein. From others spring forth vast, intricate and infinitely splendid panoramas composed of peaceful and wrathful deities which, dissolving into light-rays, stream back into the glowing syllables. No words can convey the splendour of these images, but trying to visualise them without imbuing them with mantric energy would produce but pallid counterparts of what the yogins are able to conjure forth when, after training that usually involves spending many years in utter solitude, they have refined their contemplative powers and fully mastered the practice of mantric evocation. By then, their minds have become like filaments without which, though one dwells close to a source of electric power, one's house remains in darkness.

It would not do to suppose that this splendid psychedelic imagery is to be sought and enjoyed for its own sake. All that wealth of shining colours, the juggling with space that reduces worlds to the size of pebbles, have no point to them unless they lead to full realisation of the Void. The yogin must come to perceive that he himself and all the universes he beholds are devoid of the smallest trace of own-being. He must experience the relativity of vast and tiny, the interpenetration and ultimate identity of all objects and, above all, *samsara*'s essential void-non-voidness. Thus is the mind prepared for the ultimate consummation – liberation from the spell of that master of magicians, the ego, attainment of the bliss of realised union, Enlightenment, Nirvana!

If, as I fear, these words fail to inspire holy awe, the fault is mine. I still have far to go and cannot write of the higher mysteries from direct experience. However, I did not undertake to set forth the Sublime Mystery itself, but only one of the means for its attainment. A book describing the equipment used by Himalayan climbers is a poor substitute for beholding the dazzling snow-peaks of that loveliest and most sacred of all mountains, Kanchenjunga!

Chapter 5

Some Yogic Mantras

Once while circumambulating the great stupa (*chetiya*) in the ancient city of Nakorn Pathom in central Thailand – a vast yet exquisitely graceful building, of which the massive spire and stupendous dome are faced with tiles the colour of sunshine – I came upon a sight so unexpected that I stood entranced. It was as though a mound of Kanchenjunga's snow had been transported to that torrid, shimmering plain! There in the lush gardens beyond the stupa's western face, lay an ornamental pool from the centre of which rose a statue of Padma Sambhava, the Lotus-Born, the 'Precious Guru' of the Nyingmapas! In a country where the Tibetan form of Buddhism is virtually unknown and the Nyingma Sect unheard of, encountering a statue of this being was almost as wondrous as beholding a figure of the Virgin in Mecca! Thunderstruck, I gazed and gazed, while memories rushed upon me. Almost I could hear the clash and roll of cymbals and the thrilling sound of Tibetan ritual drums. For me the scent of frangipani was magically transmuted to the fragrance of Tibetan incense touched with the sharper tang of smoke from butter-lamps. To my inner ear came the chanting of the Precious Guru's mantra swelling like a paean, as at some great Tibetan gathering where verses are recited in his honour and a thousand voices join in the mantra OṀ ĀḢ HŪṀ VAJRA GURU PADMA SIDDHI HŪṀ! These memories in turn evoked a sea of benevolent Tibetan faces lit with rapture.

Living in a city where dawn is heralded by a fleet of ten-wheel lorries revving their engines in the compound just opposite my bedroom window, I rejoice in such reminders of a majestically lovely region of the earth where silence lies upon the hills and a vigorous mystical tradition still survives – a tradition not confined, as in Japan, to temples forming islands of tranquillity ringed by the deafening clamour of this modern age, but one that is shared by all the peoples of Tibetan stock inhabiting the hills and valleys that lie within the shadow of towering Himalayan snow-peaks.

In that blessed region still unpolluted by the stench of petrol and the litter of plastic bags, one finds not only holy lamas but countless laymen in various walks of life who are not deterred by the harshness of their struggle for existence from following the path of yogic cultivation. There, yoga still retains its proper connotation – 'union'. This is a far cry from the system of gymnastic exercises comparable to judo or karate which often passes for yoga in the West. Physical exercises may be included – very exciting ones such as the generation of inner heat which enables adepts to sit naked in the snow and melt ice that is brought in contact with their flesh – but essentially theirs is a yoga that takes place in the mind, its purpose nothing less than the exalted mystical experience known to Buddhists as Supreme Enlightenment. Much of it consists of contemplative practices such as Yidam yoga of which the only physical components are the accompanying recitations and sacred postures. The psycho-physical yogas for attuning 'breathing, psychic channels and vitality' to the task of attaining Enlightenment in this very life are taught only to advanced adepts and the teaching is strictly confined to selected initiates. What are now to be described are the contemplative yogas into which it is comparatively easy to gain initiation; the mantras involved have already appeared in published works and can no longer be regarded as secret, although some of the higher uses to which they are put pertain to sacred knowledge to which access is still carefully guarded. Well above the level of what might be called popular Buddhism, they are nevertheless rather widely practised in a region where lamas empowered to bestow initiations are not hard to find. The yoga of the indwelling deity generally forms the core of the ordinary Tibetan lay initiate's practice, but seldom the whole; it is likely that his lama will require of him the performance of certain supplementary yogas in the course of which meditation deities other than the Yidam are visualised and other mantras used. This contemplation of more than one deity has, rather absurdly, given rise to a charge that the Vajrayana is polytheistic! Nothing could be further from the truth, for initiates are perfectly aware that there is ultimately only the one source of intuitive wisdom; the embodiment of this Source, or of its emanations, in various forms is due to recognition that the differentiated emanations of supreme wisdom–compassion energy can be grasped more easily by minds still far from Enlightenment. In time one discovers that there are sound psychological reasons for many aspects of yogic practice which may seem at first to be of doubtful value.

Supportive Mantras

Even prior to initiation, most Tibetans will probably have taken part in rites centring upon the mantra of compassion, OṂ MAṆI PADME HŪṂ, especially those communal evocations of Avalokiteshvara Bodhisattva during which aspirations for the well-being of individuals, groups of people or sentient beings in general are imbued by the mantra with a power that brings about some alleviation of their sufferings. Of a somewhat different kind are what may be termed 'supportive mantras', since they are used in connection with a large number of yogas in a peripheral manner.

Of particular importance is OṂ ĀḤ HŪṂ.

These are syllables of great power, the first and third so pregnant with meaning that many pages would be required to elucidate this mantra exhaustively. Employed as a 'supportive mantra', it has three major functions: (1) to create a ritually pure atmosphere prior to embarking upon the main practice; (2) to transmute material offerings into their spiritual counterparts; and (3) to compensate for a mantra one has forgotten or does not know. In this context, OṂ, the initial syllable of almost all mantras, embodies (as always) tremendous creative power and represents the Infinite, the One Mind, the all-embracing consciousness which is the very essence of existence. ĀḤ maintains, preserves what OM creates. HŪM imbues what has been created with vital energy, besides subduing passion and destroying dualistic thought. It is concentrated power devoid of ego. Together the three syllables prepare and purify the adept's mind for the yoga he is about to perform. In making offerings as part of the ancient ritual which governs yogas of this kind, their purpose being to symbolise renunciation of mundane desires, the adept inserts the name of the substance offered between the first and second syllables of the mantra, thus – OM PUSHPÉ ĀH HŪM, OM DHUPE ĀH HŪM, wherein the words inserted signify flowers and incense. As a replacement for the correct mantra with which to salute a particular mediation deity, the mantra requires the insertion of that deity's name, thus:– OM SAMANTABHADRA ĀH HŪM. Mantras thus composed can be employed to transpose the 'energy' of the deities named to the various psychic centres (*chakra*) of the adept's body. During certain contemplative rites, a white OM is seen upon the deity's brow, a red ĀH blazes at his throat and a blue HŪM shines from his heart; rays of coloured light proceeding from these syllables enter the corresponding parts of the adept's person, purifying his body, speech and mind or, at a deeper level, his 'breathing, psychic channels and vitality. In this case, OM represents the Dharmakaya or Mystical (Void) Body of a Fully Enlightened One; ĀH represents Sacred Speech; HŪM represents the Buddha-Mind. When used to accompany offerings, the mantra symbolises total surrender of the adept's faculties of body, speech and mind; otherwise, it signifies the adept's aspiration to attain the Buddha-like purity of those three faculties.

Just as OM ĀH HŪM purifies the adept himself, so does the mantra RAM YAM KHAM (pronounced so as to rhyme with the English word 'come') purify the place where the yoga is to be performed. The accompanying visualisation is grand and terrible. One beholds himself seated in the centre of a sacred area ringed by flames raging like the fire by which the universe is destroyed at a *kalpa*'s end; encircling the flames is a roaring black tempest like that which swirls at the ending of an eon; and beyond this lies an ocean topped with huge, violently agitated waves. Yogically this mantra seals the adept's

surroundings making them impervious to the evil influences
which grow all the more violent as success draws nigh, being
generated by agencies to which virtue is hateful – agencies with
which all experienced meditators are acquainted.

A less exacting way of purifying the yogic arena is to recite
OṂ VAJRA BHŪMI ĀH HŪṂ, wherein 'vajra' (adamantine)
denotes the non-substance of the Void – Ultimate Reality; and
'bhūmi' means simply 'ground'. By means of this mantra a
realm of spotless, shining void is conjured forth from the mind;
the power of the syllables OṂ ĀH HŪṂ imbues the vicinity
of the adept with the quality of pure voidness and he beholds
the phenomena around him in their absolute state; they are now
indistinguishable from the Great Void.

The Speech Transmutation Mantra

Initiates engaged in a course of contemplative yoga are often
required to start each day by reciting a mantra composed of
all the vowels and consonants of the Tibeto-Sanskrit alphabet,
which jointly comprise the elements of every conceivable mantra; the purpose is to bring about transmutation of the adept's
speech in the sense of yogically purifying his utterance. The
following Nyingmapa formula combines that mantra with an
introductory recitation which provides instruction for the
visualisation required:

OṂ ĀH HŪṂ!
From the tongue's RAṂ[1] comes fire which blazes forth
And forms a three-pronged vajra of red light –
Within, the Mantra of Causality
With mantric vowels and consonants around
In letters like a string of pearls. From them,
The light spreads forth in offering and wins
The gladness of the Buddhas and their sons.[2]
Contracting back, it purifies the speech
Of obscurations; thus it brings about
Speech-Vajra's[3] transmutation, whereupon

[1] RAṂ embodies the energy of fire.
[2] Sons of the Buddha is a term for faithful Buddhists.
[3] Speech-Vajra means the speech endowment which has to be yogically transmuted.

All siddhis[1] are attained. One now recites:
A Ā I Ī U Ū Ṛ Ṝ L̤ L̤̄ E AI O AU AṂ AḤ (seven times)
KA KHA GA GHA NGA CA CHA JA JHA NYA
ṬA ṬHA ḌA ḌHA ṄA TA THA DA DHA NA
PA PHA BA BHA MA YA RA LA WA
ŚA SHA SA HA KSHAḤ (seven times)
OṂ YE DHARMĀ HETU PRABHAWĀ HETUN TESHĀN
TATHĀGATO HYAVADAT TESHAÑ CA YO NIRODHA
    EVAṂ VĀDĪ
MAHĀ ŚRAMAṄAḤ SWĀHĀ (seven times)

The Mantra of the Precious Guru

Buddhists of all schools and sects take refuge daily in the Triple Gem – the Buddha, the Dharma (Doctrine) and the Saṃgha (Sacred Community). To these, followers of the Vajrayana add a fourth – the Guru. When the Refuges are recited, the Guru comes first – Namo Gurubé, Namo Buddhaya, Namo Dharmaya, Namo Sanghaya. This is to acknowledge that it is to one's own guru and to the lamas of his line stretching back to the Buddha himself that one owes one's entire knowledge of the other Refuges. As is proper with all yogic practice, reliance on the guru is absolute. Were his integrity or wisdom to be doubted, yogins would find themselves in the perilous position of men who sail along rocky coasts in unfamiliar seas without a navigator or with a navigator in whose judgement they have no confidence! The risks would be prodigious! Therefore what is known as guru yoga forms an essential part of Vajrayana yoga.

Nyingmapa lamas and those of most of the other sects teach that pupils who would enlist the sacred powers of yoga to enable them to leap from the realm of semblances to the blissful realm of pure being so that, perceiving their identity, they may dwell spontaneously in both, must first invoke the Precious Guru, Padma Sambhava, Founder of the Nyingma Line, whose form for contemplative purposes is held to embody those of all other teachers of sacred knowledge. Since the form envisaged is a mental creation personifying the first of the Four Refuges, perhaps the identity of the Precious Guru is not of vital importance to the practice. Nevertheless he is very well known to all

---

[1] Powers.

Tibetans both in legend and history. Legend has it that Padma Sambhava is so named because he first became known to men by taking apparitional birth in a giant lotus flower floating upon the waters of a lake in the land of Urgyen, which in ancient times lay somewhere in the region beyond the present northwest frontier of Tibet. Historically he is known to have been one of the first great yogins to carry the Buddha Dharma into Tibet from India (seventh century A.D.). Since that time he has been venerated as second only to the Buddha in men's hearts, being the fountainhead of the great Vajrayana Sect of Mahayana Buddhism. Indeed, in contexts where Absolute Reality is viewed as the ultimate source of all sacred knowledge, the Precious Guru's form is employed yogically to embody the Dharmakaya, the Body in which Buddha and Absolute are one and indistinguishable.

It is taught that the Precious Guru's transformation-bodies are innumerable; conventionally he is most often depicted either as a lovely youth or as a handsome, bearded young man seated in what is known in yoga as the 'kingly posture'. With the fingers of his right hand, which grasps a vajra (symbol of the adamantine non-substance of the Void), he forms the mudra of 'protection against obscurations of the Dharma'. With his left hand he holds a skull-cup (signifying renunciation) brimming with *amrta* (the nectar of immortality) surmounted by a jewelled vase filled with the same non-substance. An upright trident held in place by his left arm signifies the three realms of samsaric existence and the three heads thereon represent the three mystical Bodies of an Enlightened One, one of these being a skull to suggest the lack of attributes or voidness of the Dharmakaya. Every other detail of his form has its own symbolic meaning.

During yogic contemplation, Nyingmapas visualise all lamas of their line in the semblance of the Lotus Born, reverencing them all as successive embodiments of the Dharmakaya, holding that the quality of a guru most deserving of reverence is the power of his words to transmit the light of Absolute Reality. Therefore do they commence their meditation by creating a mental image of the Precious Guru and endowing it with life by means of the Guru's mantra, thus simultaneously paying homage to the unimaginable goal of mystical endeavour and to the line of teachers who have pointed the way to its attainment. No matter what a Nyingmapa adept's main practice may be, he must daily recite some verses of invocation to the Lotus Born and repeat the mantra some hundreds or thousands of times. Typical of the many verses of this kind are the following; they are from old texts, and have been extracted from a sādhana (contemplative rite) composed by the Venerable Chögyam Trungpa Tulku:

O Precious Guru, Buddha of Triple Time,
Master of the Holy Powers, always in Great Bliss, I bow at your feet.
Remover of all hindrances, revealing yourself in angry form to drive away delusions.
To you I pray, begging for sacred resolution.
I pray to you, Lama, Jewel of Jewels,
Grant resolution that I may eschew all thought of self.
Meaningless may mundane things henceforth appear.
Grant sacred resolution that wayward thoughts may cease.
May I comprehend my mind as the unborn, uncreate.
Grant resolution so that innate unrest is stilled.
May my mind become a fit vessel for the deeper Path.
May my attainment of Ultimate Truth be free from hindrances.
May the power of Wisdom and Compassion be perfected in me
And may I attain their union in the Buddha, the Vajra-Wielder.

To perform the yoga of the Precious Guru, early in the morning the adept seats himself in a clean and quiet place. After certain preliminaries like those which precede contemplation of the Yidam, his mind becomes serene, untroubled by extraneous thoughts. Wishing well to all beings and resolved to use whatever power he attains for the benefit of others, he visualises a calm blue lake whereon floats a giant lotus supporting lunar and solar discs within its widely opened petals. There sits the Eternal Child, Padma Sambhava, the Precious Guru, whom the adept, filled with joy and awe, recognises as the embodiment of the Dharmakaya but yet also of his teacher and of all the lamas of his line. By doing reverence to the Precious Guru, he reverences them all. Having prayed for blessing, the removal of all hindrances and the attainment of boundless spiritual power, he begins his recitation of the Guru's mantra whereby the visualised form is endowed with life-force and union with the Guru is achieved:

OṀ ĀḢ HŪṀ VAJRA GURU PADMA SIDDHI HŪṀ!

In the Venerable Chogyam Trungpa Tulku's translation the inner significance of these syllables is given as follows:

OṀ is the Origin, the Dharmakaya
ĀḢ is the inspiration, the Sambhogakaya
HŪM is the expression, the Nirmanakaya
VAJRA is the union of these three
GURU is the inner wisom that instructs, the central point of the mandala
PADMA is fearless compassion
SIDDHI is the·power of the Dharma Realm
HŪM is the oneness of these qualities in us

As the vision of the Precious Guru vanishes, a state of objectless awareness supervenes, whereafter follow certain aspirations and a dedication of the merit just attained to the welfare of all beings.

The Precious Guru is the supreme embodiment of tantric power whereby, emancipating oneself from the clutch of dualistic thought, one is able to employ *all* energies, whether good or bad in origin, for the swift achievement of Enlightenment. He is said to have practised meditation using piled corpses for his seat and to have transmuted the flesh of corpses into pure food, which is perhaps a forceful allegory to illustrate the process of transmuting unclean into clean. The same may be true of the story of his being transformed into the syllable HŪM and then swallowed by a fierce *dakini*, in whose body he received initiation and was cleansed of all defilements. Such imagery may be deemed revolting; but unless beauty and ugliness are accepted impartially, how can dualistic thought be overcome?

The Mantras of the Terrible Divinities
The Yidam chosen for a pupil at the time of his initiation is not always a lovely being such as Tara. In accordance with circumstances, one of the terrible divinities may be chosen, such as Yamāntaka – a horrifying transformation-body of that gentle patron of wisdom and learning, Manjushri Bodhisattva. Indeed,

each of the peaceful meditation deities has a terrifying counterpart, without which there could be no freedom from the 'good'
and 'bad' of dualistic thought. Even the gentle Tara may at
times appear as a *dakini* or female deity of ferocious mien. Contemplating deities in their horrific forms is a means of obtaining
the tremendous power needed to destroy all ego-hindrances –
passions, cravings, ignorance-born delusions, as well as of
negating the dualism involved in preference for forms that are
pleasant to behold.

No one unaware of the special characteristics of the Vajrayana
would be likely to surmise that the fiendish-looking Yamāntaka
is no other than the charming, sweet-voiced youth, Manjushri!
Of blue complexion, many-headed (the largest head that of a
ferocious bull, the smallest a tiny smiling Buddha-head at the
apex of them all which alone hints that his function is secretly
benign), Yamāntaka has countless limbs; those of his hands
which do not grasp one or another of a varied armoury of mur-
derous weapons hold such grisly objects as a goblet of blood
fashioned from a human skull; beneath his feet lie mounds of
corpses; his ornaments are wrought of bones, skulls and severed
heads; flames spout from his body in all directions – and yet,
though accomplished yogins behold him as a ravening, raging
living being surrounded by blazing fire, his nearness does not
daunt them, for they well know that his ferocity is not directed
at erring human beings, but at the evil propensities in their
minds and at the ego which must be ruthlessly destroyed before
Enlightenment can be won. He is the embodiment of their
passions, lusts and delusions, but also of the marvellous powers
of transmutation whereby the energy generated by those evils
is used and turned against them. His weapons with their sharp
and jagged blades are the instruments wherewith wisdom severs
the bonds of darkness; the hideous necklace that dangles from
his neck is composed of heads not of slaughtered humans but
of decapitated passions.

Followers of less grisly-seeming traditions are apt to argue
that there is no need for a symbolism so bestial, but more than
mere symbolism is involved; the yogin must experience those
dreadful forms as living realities fraught with fierce energy and
movement; he must, as it were, smell that bull-like odour and

feel the scorching breath of the flames as part of a tremendous psychic experience whereby, day after day, the forces of the ego are routed. It is not a matter of looking at mere pictures or meditating upon vague, lifeless forms. The Source–Reality, though ultimately calm, remote, intangible, gives rise to every kind of violent contrast in the realm of appearances. How can these be disregarded by those who seek to know Truth as a whole? Moreover, since the human consciousness contains so much that is egoistic, violent, cruel, all deeply rooted, how can those evil tendencies be countered unless by forces as ruthless and implacable as themselves? To destroy them within the space of a single life-span is a task not for the squeamish but for indomitable giants who have conquered fear and abhorrence.

Yamāntaka, whose name means Conqueror of Death, is so named because contemplation of his form by yogins properly instructed is one of the powerful means whereby the eon-long chain of birth and death is suddenly cut short. By ridding the mind of duality, both life and death are transcended; but the dark proclivities lurking in the depths of the adept's consciousness have first to be brought into the open, recognised for what they are and *then* destroyed. The deity's yogic form simultaneously portrays the hideousness of evil and the fiery energy and ferocious will-power needed for its swift destruction. Contemplation of such peaceful forms as those of Chenresig or Tara is an insufficient remedy for the grip of turgid lust or passion; hence the absolute yogic need for such beings as Yamāntaka and the terrible naked *dakinis*.

When Yamāntaka is evoked, there must be a fierce resolution to quench the triple fires of passion, lust and ignorance. The mantra whereby his form is imbued with life runs: OM YAMĀNTAKA HŪM PHAT! The mantras of fighting deities are brief! Of these syllables, only PHAT (pronounced PÉ in Tibetan) requires explanation. Its sharp, explosive ejaculation drives off evil influences, recalls a distracted mind to one-pointedness during contemplative yoga, and is a stimulus to spiritual insight. This form of yoga, like all the others, must end with a feeling of heart-felt gratitude for the power received and be followed by the dedication of merit to all beings.

The Mantra of Wisdom and Learning

Just as Avalokiteshvara personifies compassion, so Yamāntaka's benign and charming counterpart, Manjushri, personifies wisdom. The weapon he holds aloft is not one to be feared; it is the Sword of Discriminating Knowledge whereby the bonds of ignorance are severed. His other attribute, a book or a pile of volumes, represents the Perfection of Wisdom Sutras, which many Tibetans esteem above all others. Sometimes Manjushri is seen sitting cross-legged upon a lotus; more often he bestrides a handsome, friendly looking tiger. The only reminder of his wrathful emanation is his blue complexion. By Nyingmapas he is rarely taken as a Yidam, for he is believed to be elusive and hard to woo by the usual kind of invocation; yet presumably the Gelugpas think otherwise, for he and Yamāntaka are the principal guardians of their sect. There are occasions when it is exceedingly appropriate to seek his aid. As the patron of learning as well as the embodiment of wisdom, he is generally invoked by writers embarking upon new works in the fields of arts and of scientific knowledge. Many books commence with some verses in his honour, this being deemed a safeguard against grave error. His mantra runs: OM ARAPACHANA DHI. It has the peculiarity that, after being uttered thus several times, it is then uttered with multiple repetition of the final syllable, becoming OM ARAPACANA DHĪH DHĪH DHĪH DHĪH DHĪH . . . As with all mantras, mind is the King. There must be powerful aspiration for the stream of wisdom to flow from within and a feeling of heart-felt gratitude when the flow is mentally perceived.

The Mantra of Purification

A mantra with which every initiate is familiar is that of Vajrasattva, supreme embodiment of wisdom–compassion energy, who is depicted at the very centre of the mandala or schematic pattern which illustrates the divisions and subdivisions of that energy; he thus represents the Buddha Wisdom in its pure, undifferentiated form. Since even the most devoted adepts can scarcely avoid occasional infringement of the samaya-vows taken at the time of initiation, it is necessary to have means of repairing the damage. This is done by visualising Vajrasattva as seated above one's head. After suitable invocations and the generation of true repentance for what has been done amiss, one recites his Hundred Syllable Mantra again and again, during which gleaming white nectar pours from the deity's heart through the crown of the adept's head, gradually filling his whole body and expelling from his lower orifices black streams of evil propensities which flow into the gaping mouths of Yama (Death) and his minions assembled in a deep subterranean place directly below where he sits performing this cleansing rite. When, after a period that may in some cases be uncomfortably long, the adept yogically perceives that his body has been cleansed and now shines like a crystal vase brimming with pure white nectar, he desists from reciting the Hundred Word Mantra and begins the recitation of Vajrasattva's heart-mantra, which runs: OM VAJRASATTVA HŪM. These syllables now flash around him emitting rays of brilliantly coloured light – a white OM to the front, a yellow VAJRA to his right, a red SAT behind, a green TVA to his left and a blue HŪM in his heart. Continuing this practice for as long as possible, the adept concludes the rite in the usual way which culminates in a dedication of merit.

Every one of these practices depends on recognition that, throughout the entire universe, all seeming objects are born of mind. That mentally created syllables can fill the sky with a host of shining deities is because, just as the Void (the Tao, the Godhead, Mind, the Mother of the Universe) is the source, container and life of all phenomena, so is each individual mind the container of the Void! Being of one nature and unbound by spatial laws, they are coterminous. All holiness and wisdom lie within. Man's true nature transcends the highest conception of divinity ever formulated in this or other worlds. Within the compass of his skull whole galaxies revolve. Unfettered by time and space, the Vast Container of universes as numerous as grains of sand in the Ganges river is present in its entirety within the minutest of its parts!

But minds deluded by dualistic thought are blind to their true nature; and mere intellectual acceptance of the truth does nothing towards direct perception of its splendour. Therefore have various skilful means been devised to nourish clear perception. The mantras, gestures and visualisations employed in these yogas give access to psychic factors embedded at the deepest level of the adept's consciousness. Men illiterate or deeply learned, superstitious or relatively enlightened, can use them with equal profit, except that the learned may have to battle with a heavier load of obscurations than the simple man.

Herein lies the true significance of mantras. Though they may perhaps be used effectively to accomplish a variety of ends, their highest purpose is to assist the mantra-wielder to come face to face with his own divinity. By comparison, all other ends are trivial.

Chapter 6

Words of Power

In the foregoing chapters, besides describing how I was drawn
into a milieu where mantric arts still flourish, I have dwelt
chiefly upon the *function* of mantras, while saying little about
their *nature*. I have established that, among Tibetans, their pri-
mary function relates to contemplative yoga; and I have
touched upon their use to achieve results apparently external
to the mantra-wielder's mind such as the alleviation of illness,
but suggested that their operation in such cases may be more
subjective than at first appears. I have also mentioned, though
not investigated, the claims put forward by many Tibetans that
mantras can indeed achieve miraculous results, such as causing
or averting hail-storms. For the moment I shall leave this third
possibility aside and be content with the two assertions that
mantras can be used yogically with astonishing effect, and that
they sometimes appear to operate in a manner partly or wholly
objective. Two questions now arise:

*What is the nature of mantras and the true explanation of their
power?*

*If, as is often supposed, it is sheer faith in a mantra's efficacy
that imbues it with power, is there really need for a wide range
of mantras; would not ANY mantra bring about every one of the
results achievable, if a properly trained mantra-wielder were convinced of its efficacy for all purposes?*

The precise nature of mantras is a matter so difficult to arrive
at that I have thought it best to begin by reviewing the subject
in a global context, for there are few communities in the world
wherein widespread belief in the creative and transforming

powers of sound has never taken root. The Hindu doctrine regarding the mighty force of *shabda* (sacred sound), which is taught by some sects to this day, has ancient parallels in such concepts as the Logos, the harmony of the spheres and so on. Possibly the dictum uttered by Confucius some two and a half millenia ago to the effect that music is essential to the proper governance of the state possesses a more transcendental significance than it is generally accorded. There are in the writings of the ancients many curious passages attributing stupendous or even supreme creative power to the divine energy of sound. In later writings, such passages grow sparser; except among certain Hindu tantric sects, belief that a supreme sound energy brought about the universe's creation recedes; but remnants of that belief or of others analogous to it linger in the attribution of creative, transforming or destructive power to esoteric utterances ranging from mantras to magicians' spells. Some random examples, both past and present, follow:

There is a cabbalistic figure of the Tree of Life which, representing the universe, has twenty-two limbs each of which stands for a letter of the Hebrew alphabet, to which is attributed a corresponding hierarchy of ideas. The notion of the sounds of an alphabet magically representing the totality of wisdom is reminiscent of the Tibetan Speech Transmutation Mantra already described. From G. R. S. Mead we learn that the Mithraic liturgy contained magical formulas held to be 'root-sounds' that give birth to certain divine powers. The term 'root-sounds' immediately calls to mind the Hindu and Buddhist bija-mantras, for '*bija*' means 'seed'. Novalis tells us that the speech of the novices of Sais was a wondrous song whose tones penetrated nature's inwardness, 'splitting it apart' and whose vibrations 'called forth images of all the world's phenomena'. The evocation of images is precisely the function of the mantras used in contemplative yoga; and the splitting apart of entities in response to words of power may have a bearing on the view put forward in the next chapter that every object is related to a subtle sound which, when uttered, can destroy, modify or bring into being the corresponding object. If there are really yogins with the power of shattering objects by ejaculating appropriate mantras, the secret must lie in the response of the objects shattered to some subtle counterpart of physical vibration. A reversal of this magical process would account for the calling into being of objects from thin air. I feel bound to mention these possibilities, though by no means convinced that, even supposing miracles do occur, the explanation lies in this direction.

The profound and perhaps rarely understood opening passage of the Gospel of St John does not stand alone as testimony to the existence of a once prevalent belief that the universe was born of sound; to this day one may find in India those who assert that the universe sprang forth in response to the creative syllable OM and, in ancient times, there were probably many cultures in which similar beliefs held sway. Scattered through the works of the Greek gnostics are passages which lead to that conclusion, and the liturgies of the Christian churches contain what appear to be distinct, albeit rather trifling, remnants of knowledge concerning the subtle qualities of sound. The tumbling of the walls of Jericho has sometimes been viewed in this light and it is not rare to find people who affirm that 'amen' and 'alleluia' have (or once had) a mantric significance. Certainly it is strange that these words are left untranslated in contexts wherein almost everything else has been rendered into a modern tongue. If no mantra-like virtue was ever attached to the *sound* of 'amen' (which the Encyclopedia Britannica asserts to be nothing more than a term of agreement, confirmation or desire), there would be no reason for not translating it. I have heard it suggested that, in the liturgy of the Greek Orthodox Church, where it appears in the form *'arameen'* or *'ahmeen'*, its use is closely akin to that of mantras. The case of 'alleluia' is somewhat similar; since ostensibly it means no more than 'Praise unto Ya' (Yaveh, the Lord), its retention in the original form suggests that virtue is deemed to be inherent in its sound.

Does the Hebrew custom of never pronouncing the deity's true name reflect fear of the power of sacred words? Perhaps it is merely respectful, like the Chinese avoidance of words that happen to form part of one's father's name, even though they be such commonly used words as *'kuang'* (light) or *'wên'* (literature). On the other hand, it might be due to belief that God's true name is a word of dire power that might blast the user – a concept which also has a Chinese counterpart which is exemplified by the deliberate mispronunciation of the word for 'four' in Cantonese because of its being a homonym of the term for 'death' – a word of ill-omen whose utterance might entail fatal consequences.

Then again, one wonders why the Catholic Church enjoins *multiple* repetitions of prayers such as the Pater Noster and Ave Maria, if the utterance has no significance apart from the meaning; for meaning, far from being enhanced by repetition, is dulled thereby. Is there perhaps some trace of feeling for the power of sound to be discerned in the dismay aroused in some Catholics by the recently introduced custom of reciting Mass in the vernacular instead of in Latin? Is some of the sacrament's virtue deemed to have departed in the wake of the familiar Latin sounds? Within the fold of Islam, does the dervish custom of reciting Allah's name for hours on end derive from a belief in the virtue of the *sound* of the holy name? To deduce from these examples vestiges of a once widespread recognition of mantric power may be going too far, but one cannot help wondering.

Stories of witchcraft and magic make much of words of power – '*abracadabra*' being but one of a host of spells to which miraculous effects are attributed. That the spells were often intended to accomplish unworthy ends makes no difference to the underlying principle. Moreover, witchcraft often flourishes as a remnant of a once-respected religion debased by long suppression and by the consequent replacement of its ordained ministers by barely literate peasants dwelling in places remote from the seats of learning and authority, so it may be that some so-called magic spells derive from sacred words of power. Neither mantras nor spells can be good or evil in themselves; like swords, they may be turned to purposes either good or ill; such efficacy as they have must depend on a mental accompaniment, for it would be ludicrous to suppose that words uttered mindlessly could be any more effective than a child's attempt to hasten a traffic-light's change to green by shouting '*Abracadabra*'. However, that is not to say that the words employed have no bearing on the issue; for, unless their utterance is a source or vehicle of power, why should there be spells at all?

All the friends to whom I wrote inquiring about Western analogies to Buddhist and Hindu mantras cited the use of the Jesus

Prayer by the more mystically inclined adherents of the Greek and Russian branches of the Orthodox Church. Personally, I consider that prayer to be less akin to mantras than to the *nien-fu* (*nembutsu* or *japa*) formulas earlier described. Yet since it is likely that these formulas operate in much the same way as mantras and draw their power from a common source, the Jesus Prayer is of great interest in this context. I am grateful to Dom Sylvester Houédard for the erudite notes from which the following brief remarks have been culled.

The Jesus Prayer is a mystical formula which runs: 'Lord Jesus Christ, Son of God, have mercy on us' (the words 'on us' being sometimes replaced by 'on me, a sinner'). Whether or not as a result of Sufi inspiration or possibly of a more indirect influence stemming from a Hindu or Buddhist source, it has been employed on Mount Athos with such yogic accompaniments as concentration on the breath and on the heart-beats, eye-fixing and evocation of inner light; often it is used more simply as a focus for yogic concentration, being recited silently or aloud *without interruption*. Of the many references to this prayer in the writings of Christian mystics, there is one by the Pseudo-Chrysostom that immediately calls to mind Yidam yoga. It runs in part:

From morning to night repeat ... (the Jesus Prayer)
While eating, drinking and so forth
Until it penetrates the heart,
Descends to the depths of the heart ...
The heart to absorb the Lord,
The Lord to absorb the heart
Until they become one.
You yourself are the temple and the place
In which to practise the prayer.

A delightful account of the traditional use of this prayer (without the special accompaniments mentioned above) is contained in the autobiography of a simple Russian mystic who made it the centre of his life; this book has been translated into English by R. M. French under the title 'The Way of a Pilgrim'. Many years have passed since I read it; but, if my memory is to be trusted, the pilgrim set himself to reciting the prayer day and night without interruption, so that it continued in his mind even when he conversed with others or attended to the business of living. His account of the marvellous results tallies closely with what Chinese or Japanese devotees have written about the invocation to Amitabha Buddha. Reading what he has to say is sufficient to disabuse one of the notion that repetition of a single formula day in and day out, year after year, is a sterile practice, much less a demented one. One can easily sense in him the sweetness, other-worldliness, latent strength and exalted spiritual attainment that made me feel joyously humble in the presence of the more saintly of Amitabha Buddha's devotees.

To Dom Sylvester I also owe the following information about a somewhat similar formula employed by Sufis seeking mystical communion with God. It is known as the Ismu'z Zat (Name of the Divine Essence) and one version of it runs: 'Hu El-Haiy El-Quaiyum' (He, the Living, the Self-Subsistent). While this is reminiscent of the *nien-fu* formulas, there are also Sufis who recite the syllable 'Hu' or 'Huwa' alone, silently or aloud without interruption, a practice so close to the Hindu recitation of the mantric syllable OM that one begins to wonder whether it is proper to draw a distinction between *nien-fu* and mantric practice.

In recent years, sufficient interest in the Hindu and Buddhist use of mantras has arisen for the Sanskrit term 'mantra' to have passed into the English language, but it is often used rather loosely. Properly speaking, mantras, in contradistinction to other sacred invocations (which may, however, be held to operate mantrically), are arrangements of sacred syllables, varying from one to several thousand syllables, whose efficacy depends not at all upon their verbal meaning, even if some sort of meaning can be derived from them. OM MANI PADME HŪM is a good example of a mantra of which all but the first and last syllables do have a verbal meaning, but not one that gives more than a vague clue to its true import.

Even in those parts of the Buddhist world where Vajrayana influence has been virtually nil, forms of mantric or quasi-mantric practice are used a great deal more often than many

Western converts to Buddhism suppose. Even the Ch'an (Zen) Sect, which is often depicted by Western writers as being sternly opposed to rites, recitations and other liturgical practices, does in fact employ mantras; for example, Ch'an monks daily recite the Smaller Heart Sutra, a work of immense profundity, which ends with the words: GATÉ GATÉ PĀRAGATÉ PĀRASAMGATÉ BODHI SVĀHĀ. This is described in that sutra as 'the unequalled mantra, the allayer of all suffering' and, though it has a more or less intelligible meaning (Gone, gone, gone beyond, gone wholly beyond – Enlightenment!) it is used like other mantras without reference to its sense, being in fact an invocation of Prajñāpāramitā, embodiment of transcendental wisdom. Similarly it makes only superficial sense to speak of the Theravadin Buddhists of Southeast Asia as setting no store by mantras. The Mangala Sutra chanted at weddings, housewarmings and on other joyful occasions is one of several texts whose recitation is held to be auspicious, productive of good fortune. These and the Parittas recited to banish illness, without being exactly mantras, are highly esteemed for their mantric effect. So in a way is the daily recited formula of taking refuge in the Triple Gem, which is invariably chanted *thrice*. The stress on multiple recitation of sacred formulas indicates that some virtue over and above the meaning conveyed is attached to them, that they are believed to bestow blessing or ward off evil; in other words that they have the very qualities that are *popularly* attributed to mantras. That this attribution of mantra-like power is not (or formerly was not) altogether unconscious is borne out by the fact that Thai Theravadins use the term *'suat mon'* (meaning literally 'reciting mantras') when referring to this practice, *'mon'* being the Thai contraction of the word 'mantra'. The use of mantras or of other verbal formulas held to be imbued with power is a characteristic of those types of religious practice which are inspired by doctrines that are essentially mystical.

Of the three categories into which I tend to divide mantras – namely those subjective, apparently objective and actually objective in their manner of operation, it is certain that the first and probable that the second do in fact operate by means of creative, transforming and destructive processes that take place *within the mantra-wielder's own mind.* It is only those within the third category that have a more than superficial resemblance to magic spells. Of the other two, the first category is over-whelmingly important. Nowadays at least, the teaching of the lamas on the subject of mantras is almost wholly concerned with their use in contemplative yoga; they tend to dismiss other uses as being too unimportant to merit sustained attention – not because belief in what might well be called supernatural pheno-mena has diminished, but simply on account of their singleminded concern for the rapid spiritual development of their pupils. At the popular level, however, Tibetans take an immense interest in what are or appear to be objective effects achievable by mantras, which are probably regarded as being more or less identical with magic spells. One hears a great deal of mantras being used to ward off dangers and misfortunes, but few people seem to have given any thought to the question as to whether the mantra-wielder attains invulnerability to certain ills by bringing about a transformation within himself or whether he can actually cause transformations to external objects or circumstances.

It does not do to pour scorn on these popular beliefs. There is more than sufficient evidence to indicate that some of the 'external' effects claimed for mantras really do occur. The facts are there, but, whatever stance one takes towards them, certain aspects remain puzzling. For example, there can be no doubt whatever that mantras are sometimes effective in curing illness, whether one's own or another's. This I know from first-hand experience, having both undergone and witnessed if not cures, then alleviations of illness wrought by mantras. Yet there are lamas highly renowned for yogic skills who suffer severely from recurring maladies such as asthma, which I believe is a com-plaint sufficiently 'psychosomatic' in character to be amenable to subjective treatment. Why do they not cure themselves yogically? Is it because they *cannot* or because they are deterred from doing so by their intimate knowledge of the operation of karmic law, by a conviction that, if suffering is due, to dispel it in one form would simply be to court it in another?

Of mantras employed for coping with a wide variety of ills, those of the Twenty-One Taras offer a comprehensive example.

I have heard too many well-attested accounts of their effectiveness to doubt them all, yet I find it very difficult to accept that mantras can cause fire, flood or tempest to subside, or soldiers – though possibly demons – to relinquish their fell designs. However, I have occasionally come across scientific articles that may be relevant to the matter. According to some authorities, *all* illness is fundamentally psychosomatic; if that is so, then mantric cures are less to be wondered at. Then again there is the concept of 'accident-proneness' which relates unpleasant encounters with external circumstances to states of mind. When we know more about what is involved in altering an individual's degree of proneness to accidents, we may begin to glimpse the principles underlying the operation of the mantras of the Twenty-One Taras. Meanwhile one must seek some kind of explanation, that is neither full nor particularised, in the mystical conception of mind as the ground, container and being of all phenomena. When this view is accepted, the most spectacular mysteries cease to astonish – or, rather, the most trivial objects and circumstances are revealed as mysteries of the highest order, with the result that nothing of which the mind can conceive seems altogether improbable.

In reading about and talking with Tibetans, one often comes across references to what are commonly regarded as supernormal powers. That such powers can be developed is something I have long accepted; for, though they are rarely if ever displayed for the purpose of demonstrating their existence, one cannot help stumbling upon examples of them when living among people with advanced yogic training. The most widespread and frequently witnessed of these is the power of telepathy; without particularly meaning to do so, many gifted lamas display in dealing with their pupils a disconcerting ability to read thoughts that have not yet been put into words, including thoughts that one would not dream of voicing even if given the opportunity! This should not seem strange. If devoting one's whole life to arduous yogic practice failed to produce remarkable fruits, the Tibetans – a highly practical people – would have abandoned their ascetic practices centuries ago. In matters of this kind, it is of course difficult to pinpoint the precise significance of mantras, since they are but one of the many factors involved in yogic training and cannot be divorced from the psychic processes that accompany their utterance.

However far one may go in attempting to explain matters in subjective terms, one is left with a hard core of mantric effects that cannot be thus explained; either one must refuse to credit that they sometimes occur, or else accept them as miraculous. This, from a non-yogic point of view, is the most intriguing aspect of the whole subject. In the works of some of the earlier Christian missionaries who wrote accounts of the Himalayan region and of Tibet itself can be found descriptions of such extraordinary occurrences as the vanishing, transformation or multiplication of material objects in response to mantric utterances; and I came across a rather similar account written not many years ago by a member of a Seventh Day Adventist mission (or a Jehovah's Witness – I cannot recall which). Moreover, there are innumerable Tibetan accounts of lamas capable of such feats as creating animated replicas of their own bodies in order to appear in two widely separated localities simultaneously. Nor must one overlook those passages in the biography of the great poet-sage Milarepa that describe miraculous occurrences, such as his evoking a hail-storm, during his unregenerate days, that destroyed the persecutors of his family. Indeed I have met a good many people, not all of them Tibetans, who claim to have witnessed the summoning or dispersal of rain-clouds by mantric skill; one was the Indian Resident in Sikkim some years ago, a man widely known for his sagacity and erudition and not at all the sort of person who invents or relay stories of miracles just for the sake of impressing his audience. I never heard my lamas dismiss such occurrences as being unworthy of credence; I believe their reluctance to discuss them with me was due only to a feeling that my curiosity was a trifle reprehensible, like that of a visitor who, having been offered pearls and jade, insists on urging his hosts to bring out some ingenious little toys for his entertainment. Courteously turning aside my questions, they left me wondering.

Since my lamas, whose wisdom was undoubted, almost certainly believed that external objects can be acted upon and even transformed by mantric power, I feel there must be some grounds for that belief. Theoretically, of course, it implies that an accomplished yogin pursued by a tiger could cause the beast to diminish to the size of a kitten or vanish altogether! Well, my credulity does not stretch *that* far, and yet I have actually witnessed something (admittedly much less sensational) akin to such a feat; that is, I once saw an angry, snapping dog turn suddenly and slink away, its tail between its legs, in response to a softly intoned mantra unaccompanied by anything in the nature of a threatening noise or gesture! So I am left in the position of tentatively accepting a principle but rejecting some of its implications. Perhaps I ought not to reject them; my firm conviction that the universe is a mental creation ought logically to carry with it recognition that nothing in the whole realm of objective phenomena is truly impossible to an adept skilled in manipulating mental creations. However, the furthest I can go in that direction is to avoid shutting my mind very firmly against any possibility merely on the grounds that it strikes me as bizarre.

It was natural for my lamas to discourage mere curiosity or academic interest in such matters; they held that a student of yoga should be fully occupied with making practical use of what he has learnt. This obliged me to depend on chance observation or even upon mere speculation. In the next chapter, I offer – very tentatively – the suggestions that really extraordinary mantric feats may require a mastery of the laws of *shabda* (sacred sound); and that possibly most lamas are not fully acquainted with those laws or, at all events, not prepared to discuss them; the former would explain why conjuring objects from thin air or causing them to vanish is, even if theoretically possible, rarely seen these days.

Concerning the subjective, and easily demonstrable, effects of the mantras used in contemplative yoga there is no room for doubt. One has but to learn to perform the yoga properly to discover the power of mantras for oneself. Here the only difficulty would lie in persuading meditators of other faiths to accept the exotic-looking images evoked as true embodiments of principles or psychic phenomena of the utmost sanctity. It cannot be too strongly emphasised that the ultimate mystical experience is the same for all, whether initially conceived of as union with the Godhead or as realisation of union with the Source that has never from the first been interrupted but only lost to view. Adherents of whatever faith are certain to perceive this for themselves upon reaching a sufficiently advanced stage; but, at the start and for as long as images of any kind persist, people's different concepts of the Sublime will continue to colour not only their personal beliefs but also their psychic experiences. I recall some correspondence I had recently with a European lady who wrote to me describing how, during LSD experiments undertaken with a religious object in view, she had enjoyed communion with Amitabha Buddha and with her Tibetan guru. Without presuming to question those assertions, I suggested that her experience, though very likely of a spiritual order, might have taken its specific content and colour from her previous meditation on those two beings. In many cases of early mystical experience, whether attained through yogic practice or induced by drugs or other means, one cannot be sure as to how much, if any, of the content is independent of preconceived beliefs and previously encountered imagery; it is only at the stage at which imagery is transcended that certainty is won.

Nevertheless the universality of the content of *truly profound* mystical experience, regardless of training and belief, became clear to me at an early stage of my practice. While still in China, I encountered two main forms of yogic endeavour, the one conceived of in terms of well-defined religious belief (usually in Amitabha or Kuan Yin), the other in terms of Zen-style abstractions such as the One Mind, the Great Void (or Void-non-Void), the Ultimate Source (Tao) and so on. Adherents of the former, which is called other-power yoga, generally knew from the first or presently came to recognise that the meditation Buddhas and Bodhisattvas called forth by mantras or by *nien-fu* practice were but embodiments of beneficent forces emerging from and leading back to the Ultimate Source, which itself resides in the individual's consciousness. The only real difference between them and the adherents of self-power yoga (such as Zen adepts) was that the latter prefer to seek the same goal without the help of these psychic embodiments.

Recognition of the validity and underlying identity of both these approaches should extend beyond the Buddhist fold. The Christian seeking mystical union with God employs what

Buddhists call other-power yoga, whereas Mahayana Buddhists are inclined to resort to both kinds, though with individual emphasis on the one or the other. Chinese and Tibetan teachers have too much wisdom to insist that either of the main yogic paths is intrinsically superior to the other; so much depends on the pupil's temperament and propensities. Personally I emphasise other-power yoga in my practice (unless one regards contemplative yoga as containing elements of both) simply because the use of mantras and similar aids leads to results I can seldom attain by pure self-power yoga. This is undoubtedly the chief purpose of mantras and here, at least, no 'magic' is involved. They serve that purpose until the adept nears the apex of the path, whereat all set practices are discarded or fall away of themselves.

Chapter 7

Shabda, Sacred Sound

The fact that belief in mantric power, or something closely akin to it, was once more or less world-wide may encourage one to believe in its reality, but it does nothing to elucidate the real nature of mantras. To say that the source of their power is mind carries one no further, especially if one believes, as all mantra users do, that everything conceivable derives from mind. What is more, there are a good many anecdotes current in Tibetan circles which, if taken by themselves, would lead to the conclusion that there is no need for a range of different mantras, that *one* (whether learnt or invented for one's own purposes) would be enough. Here are two of those anecdotes:

A work called the Lam-rim Zin-dr'ol Lag-chang contains an account of an Indian monk who broke his annual retreat during the rainy season to visit his mother, supposing her to be desperately short of food. Surprised to find her looking well and happy, he was even more astonished when she told him she had learnt a special mantra wherewith 'by the power of the Great Goddess', she was able to cause rocks to boil and transmute them into nourishing food; but, being a deeply learned man, he had no sooner heard her recite the mantra than he set about correcting numerous mistakes in her way of uttering it. Alas, when the poor woman recited the mantra correctly, it proved quite ineffective, whereat her son advised her to return to her former mode of recitation and soon, thanks to her great faith, she was happily changing rocks into food again!

In the She-nyan Ten-tsül Nyong-la Nä-tu K'al-wa, there is a story about a Tibetan with great faith in the wisdom of Indian gurus, but with little knowledge of Sanskrit. Travelling to India and calling upon a famous guru at an inauspicious moment, he was met with a shouted 'Go away!' and a sweeping gesture of dismissal. These he mistook for a powerful mantra with its appropriate mudra and, practising them in a mountain retreat, he soon reached a high level of attainment. On returning to the guru to give thanks, he learnt of his ludicrous mistake; but the guru, instead of upbraiding him for folly, congratulated him on having achieved valuable insights from an unconventional practice by reason of his unswerving faith!

I am sure that most Tibetan lamas share the liberal attitude to mantras revealed by these anecdotes; and yet, except in rare cases of unmatchable faith, it is hardly possible that nonsense-sounds such as ba-ba-ba or bu-bu-bu would be found effective as substitutes for mantras; otherwise, the present wide range of mantras would not have been evolved or, at all events, would not still be taught in a sequence of ascending importance. My lamas did not enlighten me regarding this matter; indeed, their single-minded devotion to their pupils' yogic progress was such that such questions soon ceased to occupy my mind. Much the same was true of my attitude towards the more spectacular or 'miraculous' uses of mantras; as my studies progressed, I thought less and less about them; for it was borne upon me that true yogins would not be greatly moved even by the sight of a raging tiger mantrically transformed before their eyes into a tiny kitten! Death comes to all in one way or another; one may escape a tiger's maw only to drown ignominiously in a puddle, whereas no one can escape wandering from birth to birth in the sad and often painful realm of delusion until he has brought about a final shattering of his ego; only such aid as mantras can give in that direction is of lasting importance. Even so it would be against nature for an ordinary person like myself to be wholly incurious as to the possibility of turning ferocious beasts into harmless – if understandably frustrated – kittens! The magical aspect of mantras has never quite lost its attraction for me; and so, in this final chapter, I shall offer some speculations regarding both the nature of mantras and the possibility that they can sometimes miraculously affect external objects, these two matters being closely bound up with each other.

There are authorities, Hindus especially (and perhaps, in

theory at least, Buddhists), who hold that mantras are manifestations of *shabda* (sacred sound), an energy with creative,
transforming and destructive powers as mighty as those attributed by theists to their God (or gods). Unfortunately, it is hard
to come upon a clear description of the nature of *shabda*. It
would be laughable to suppose, the works of several modern
writers notwithstanding, that *shabda* operates through physical
vibrations! Surely physical vibrations are a far cry from the
sublime Hindu concept of *shabda*'s creative power, which is
reminiscent of St John's resounding: 'In the beginning was the
Word . . . and the Word was God'? On the other hand, the gnos-
tic concept, Logos (the Word), must involve some kind of relationship to sound, otherwise the choice of that term would be
inexplicable. We may, I think, take it that there *is* a correspondence between *shabda* and ordinary sound, however much
exalted the one above the other. Probably it is a correspondence
similar to that which obtains between *prana-vayu* (*ch'i* in
Chinese) and the ordinary air we breathe. Though, as every
adept of the breathing yogas knows, *prana* (cosmic energy) is
drawn into the body through the pores and nostrils, common
air is nothing more than its conveyor and its crude counterpart.
Whereas both sound and the motion of the air relate to physics,
shabda and *prana* are mysterious energies whose nature can be
fully understood, if at all, only by advanced yogins.

Contemporary Western writers on Hindu and Buddhist
yogic principles seem particularly prone to a widespread misconception as to the meaning of the teaching that every being –
human, animal, divine, demonic – every substance and every
physical entity possesses its unique shabdic quality to which
can be found mantric syllables that correspond. One after
another writer has diminished *shabda*'s stature by bringing it
down to the level of electronics. Thus Dr Evans Wentz, despite
having lived with erudite Tibetan teachers, employs the term
'particular rate of vibration' to denote an object's shabdic
quality or subtle sound. More recently Philip Rawson, in
a book called 'Tantra', writes of the fabric of even the densest-
seeming objects as being 'of an order related to vibration'; so
far, so good, for it is indeed possible that a mantra's shabdic
effect on an object external to the yogin is subtly *related to* vibra-

tion, but then the writer goes on to affirm that what are experienced as differences and interactions between material things are due to 'interference-patterns produced among combined frequencies'! Well, I know too little of physics to be able to engage in polemics on this subject, but I am very sure that such a concept would astound the Tibetan exponents of mantric yoga!

Since the Lama Govinda, whose knowledge of the operation of mantras is profound, uses the term 'subtle vibration' in speaking of them, I do not venture to suggest that the term 'vibration' be altogether discarded in this connection, but I believe it should be made abundantly clear that 'subtle vibrations' must be of a *very* different order from those associated with aeroplanes! The folly of thinking in terms of something like physical vibrations can easily be demonstrated; since variants of the mantric syllable OM (e.g. UM) produce the same mantric effects, whatever vibration is involved must result from the final M; but, if that is so, how about the bija-mantras HŪM, TĀM, RAM, YAM, KHAM and most others which share that ending and yet have enormously different mantric uses? And what of those variants of OM which, though effective, do not contain that final M, e.g. UNG (Tibetan), ANG (Chinese) and ONG (Japanese)? Consider also the destructive syllable PHAT; in its Sanskrit form it even sounds destructive, yet the Chinese and Tibetans manage to use it effectively though pronouncing it more or less like PHÉ!

One need not deduce from these examples that the correlation between *shabda* and ordinary sound is insignificant; just as air is the vehicle of *prana* so may sound be the vehicle of *shabda*. That there *is* a relationship was more than once impressed on me by such experiences as being plunged into a state of exaltation while passing a Chinese mountain hermitage after sundown and hearing the resonant *bok-bok-bok* of a 'wooden-fish drum' fall upon the stillness of the night – an exaltation of somewhat the same quality as that attainable with the help of mantras. Where many people err is in attributing too much importance to the manner in which mantric syllables are uttered. I am convinced that the sound component taken in isolation from the rest normally has but little significance. Were someone uninstructed in mantric yoga to hear a mantra faultlessly recited by a veritable master among mantra-wielders and were he then to reproduce it to perfection – enunciation, rhythm, vibrations both gross and subtle – the effect would be nil! The Lama Govinda comes close to the heart of the matter in teaching that the subtle vibrations of mantras are intensified by mental associations which crystallise around them through tradition or individual experience. It follows that the manner of enunciation, though not necessarily without any importance whatsoever, is of far less consequence than the accompanying mental act. True, subtle sound when conjoined with mental power may evoke dormant forces within the mantra-wielder's mind; but whereas mental power divorced from subtle sound can in itself be highly effective, the reverse does not hold true.

Even assuming that a mantra's shabdic quality is an important component of its effectiveness, that quality can come into play only when the mantra is uttered by one properly instructed in the art of yogic visualisation; for mantras have not only sound, but also form and colour; the form or the archetypal image or symbol with which it is associated must be evoked at the moment of utterance, since that image is the repository of all the psychic, emotional and spiritual energy with which the adept has endowed it during months or years of yogic practice, together with the associated psychic energy drawn from all the adepts who have ever concentrated upon that particular image or symbol since it first came into being. (That the energy generated by a succession of yogins throughout the centuries is present in such symbols is a concept that will not surprise those acquainted with C. G. Jung's teaching about archetypes.) As set forth in the chapter on the indwelling deity, the lamas teach that the mantra appropriate to each of the divine forms contemplated embodies the psychic energy of that 'being'. In other words, the yogically visualised image of the deity or the mantric syllable that symbolises it is a centre for the powerful thought-associations built around it by countless yogins during past centuries and by the adept himself in his meditations; however, it also constitutes a particular embodiment of the energies streaming from the Source and it is to this aspect that the shabdic quality of the appropriate mantra probably pertains.

As the sound is no more than a symbol of the mantra's latent power, mispronunciation of the syllables is no grave matter, for it is the adept's *intention* that unlocks the powers of his mind. Though the mantra may consist of syllables to which no conceptual meaning is attached, pronouncing them nevertheless enables him to conjure up instantly in his mind the psychic qualities he has learnt to associate with them.

Therefore it seems plausible to suppose that the shabdic quality or power resides not in the actual sound produced but in *the archetypal sound which it represents*, for then the equal effectiveness of such variants as OM, UM, UNG, etc., becomes fully explicable – and not in terms of faith alone.

My friend, Gerald Yorke, who is deeply erudite in some categories of words of power, has brought to my attention the metaphysical concept of *shabda* that prevails in Hindu tantric circles. With his permission I have made the following brief abstract of the information put at my disposal. First, however, I must point out that, though this Hindu concept may have an important bearing on the nature of mantras, it is a grave mistake to equate Hindu and Buddhist tantric teaching very closely; the yogic traditions of the two systems are sometimes diametrically opposed even on points of key significance; furthermore, Indians, being by nature fond of metaphysical speculation, differ fundamentally from the much more pragmatic, down-to-earth Tibetans and Chinese; so that, whether or not Hindu and Buddhist tantric yoga sprang from the same source, no common conceptual basis can now be found for them.

Hindu teachers of mantric yoga are said to attach immense importance to ensuring correctness of sound and vibration; how a mantra should be uttered is kept secret from non-initiates, who are thereby effectively debarred from utilising its power. It is taught that the universe is the 'play of spirit in the ether of consciousness (chitākāsha)' and that the spirit going forth from God becomes Sound God (Shabdabrahman), the myriad objects constituting the universe being the creations of sound, or rather of *shabda*. Moreover the female (active) aspect of God can be invoked by speech, whereas the male (passive) aspect can be approached only in silence. God's creative energy gives rise to the subtle body of sound (*shabda*) which in turn becomes a wave that can be heard. In a sense the whole universe proceeds from OM – the totality of all sound. There are four planes of *shabda* – that which is neither sound nor silence but transcends them both; that which cannot be heard or even imagined but only experienced directly in a yogic state of consciousness; that which can be imagined but not heard, manifesting itself only in dream and vision; and that which is speech or mere noise. By means of the mantra OM, one can work back from this fourth plane to the first. Each noise in nature is a trinity of sound, form and perception. Each mantric syllable has a complete correspondence with the idea it represents; hence, by correct utterance of the right syllable without cogitation, one can realise the idea on ascending planes rising to God Himself.

How much, if any, of this teaching is acceptable to Tibetan yogins, I do not know. If such a doctrine does exist among them (in a form that fits the Buddhist concept of a universe with no creator-God), it must either be held too sacred for the ears of ordinary initiates or else, as seems more likely, be deemed too metaphysical to have any practical value for them. Buddhist teachers are much more concerned with the practical application of sacred knowledge than with underlying theory.

I wish I had gained a fuller knowledge of the Tibetan concept of the nature of *shabda*. My lamas did no more than mention it in passing as a component of mantric power. I have been driven to form my own hypothesis, which may or may not have some factual foundation; it relates to the distinction I drew earlier between the subjective and external operation of mantras. In the case of the former, it is abundantly clear that accuracy of pronunciation and intonation do not greatly matter, hence my conclusion that *shabda* here relates to sound *archetypes* rather than to the sound actually produced. In the case of the latter, it seems to me just possible that perfection of utterance is an ingredient essential to a mantra's operation.

Thousands of Tibetans use mantras effectively for yogic purposes every day, whereas 'magical' effects upon external objects are now rare – although, unless one discounts a good deal of evidence, they are not unknown even in this day and age. It would seem that most lamas either do not know or else prefer not to teach certain shabdic secrets pertaining to the miraculous use of mantras. If one may assume that, in former times, these secrets were more widely taught than now, that would explain why there are so many references to 'magical' mantric operations in Tibetan literature. Such a hypothesis would resolve the contradiction between the view that perfect utterance is of supreme importance and the view, based on experience of mantric effects during yogic contemplation, that it is of hardly any importance at all; for it would follow that each view is correct in relation to one set of objectives. This is an exciting thought, for one can then accept that even today there may very well be adepts who, as heirs to the secret knowledge transmitted down the ages, are capable of performing such prodigious feats as creating spirit replicas of their own bodies! It is also a comforting thought, for the insistence of one's lamas that such feats do indeed occur poses an unfortunate dilemma; either one is compelled to believe in the well-nigh unbelievable or else, since it is usually impossible to doubt the good faith of one's lamas, one must suppose them over-credulous. Of these alternatives, the first becomes possible only if some such explanation as the one I have put forward lies to hand; the second involves the paradox of attributing simple credulity to men who are quite obviously both down-to-earth and extraordinarily wise.

That the mantras employed in yogic contemplation conjure up tremendous power is as obvious to me as the heat of the sun or the wetness of rain, all being matters of direct experience; yet the nature of *shabda* remains elusive. Vague statements such as that particular sounds have shabdic affinities with particular components of consciousness on which they act leave a great deal unexplained. But then, perhaps it is best not to be greatly concerned about the reasons for a mantra's power or the manner in which it operates. Millions of people use electricity to light and warm their dwellings without understanding its nature or knowing how it functions. Life is too short for making exhaustive inquiries into everything we make use of. Nothing in this mentally created universe is ever what it seems, and it was the Buddha himself who taught that time spent in speculation as to the 'why' of things would be better spent on experiencing their 'what'. Whether rain is produced by sky-dragons, as the Chinese once thought, or by condensation of water drawn from the earth makes no difference to the *effect* of rain. Dragons or not – no rain, no crops, no life!

One does, of course, need some criterion to observe when reciting mantras, especially as faith in their efficacy is essential to success. Personally I believe that every tradition should be observed exactly in the form in which it was transmitted by one's teacher, even though, if one has had several teachers, some notable inconsistencies may result. Were I to make use of all the mantras about which I have received instruction at one time or another, I should pronounce some in the curious Sino-Japanese-Sanskrit used at the Forest of Recluses, not a few in the Chinese manner and many in the Tibetan. So be it! That way I have faith in them. The need to acquire a mode of uttering mantras in which one can have confidence is in itself a reason – perhaps the least important and yet not unimportant – for seeking initiation. The lama who bestows it will have received an oral transmission stemming from the ancient founders of his line.

A special problem for Westerners arises from the need to visualise mantric syllables correctly. I once asked the Junior Tutor of His Holiness the Dalai Lama whether the effect would be marred if the Roman equivalents of the Tibetan letters were visualised. After careful thought, the venerable lama replied: 'There can be no special virtue in the Tibetan letters, for we often visualise mantras as being composed of syllables written in one of the Indian scripts that is used for transcribing them. So, at first sight, it would seem that any script would do. However, an important feature of the Tibetan and Indian alphabets is lacking in your English script; our manner of combining consonants and vowels into single characters lends itself to the visualisation of mantric syllables withdrawing into themselves, contracting into the tiny circle at the top (e.g. ཨྲུཾ into ˚) and vanishing. I do not think that visualisation of syllables in their English form with vowels and consonants written side by side would be effective.'

One must attach great weight to the advice of so eminent an authority. Nevertheless, in the case of people who, knowing neither Sanskrit nor Tibetan, find it impossible to perform the visualisation in the traditional manner, I cannot help thinking that it would be better to visualise the English equivalents than to dispense with the practice altogether, for then their use of mantras would certainly be worthless.

When one first embarks on mantric yoga, it is natural to inquire about the meaning of the syllables, but it is better not to be greatly concerned about it, since thinking about the conceptual meaning is invariably a hindrance to yogic progress. The use of mantras belongs to the realm of no-thought with which Zen followers are familiar. One must transcend the dualism of subject and object, the deluding blandishments of logical sequence; if meaning is dwelt upon, it *gets in the way of attainment!* This point can be illustrated by analogy. In Christian church services, music often plays a considerable part; in their Buddhist equivalent, there is rarely a musical accompaniment apart from the striking of percussion instruments. Melodies, even if there are no words to them, are apt to arouse reveries – exalted perhaps, but nonetheless involving the play of thought; whereas a sudden clang or rhythmic drumming may jerk or coax the mind into the realm of no-thought. (Needless to say, 'no-thought' in this context does not denote a state of mindless torpor, a sinking of the devotee's consciousness to the level of lifeless wood or stone, but transcendence of the ordinary mode of consciousness, a leap from subject-object awareness to ecstatic perception of the non-dual.)

Writing a book on mantras has been very much like trying to catch air in a net. So often, setting out to explain a mystical doctrine or practice amounts to endeavouring to bind the ineffable – as though that were possible! The sublime brought down to the level of common sense vanishes or is diminished. In seeking to share one's knowledge, it is all too easy to fall into the error of small children who, having just learnt to tell the time, feel confident of being able to dissect and reassemble daddy's wrist-watch!

Contemplative yoga belongs to an exalted order of knowledge about which it is wiser to refrain from explanation; one may so easily excite ridicule or – what is worse – write something dangerously misleading. Yet now that people reared in a society unfamiliar with the means of gaining transcendent powers of mind are eager to explore such matters, but generally cut off from traditional sources of knowledge, misunderstandings inevitably arise, such as a belief that mantras are magic spells or that their operation is governed by the laws of physical vibration. Even with regard to yoga, one must *start* from somewhere near the level of common sense; later, as one's knowledge expands, common sense can be thrown on the gigantic rubbish heap where rusting cars, discarded tins and plastic fragments lie piled, forming a fitting monument to modern man's genius for robbing life of its mystery and depriving nature of its own.